The Trials of Jim Dunning

D.L. Ford

Keep Looking Up!

Dave E Ford

PS. 91:15

DEDICATION

This book is dedicated to my brothers and sisters in God's family who have helped me and my family along the way. Your salt and light has made the darkness of this world a little more bearable.

CONTENTS

ACKNOWLEDGMENTS

1
WHAT COMES NEXT

Bacon. Once again he was waking up to that wonderful smell of frying bacon wafting through the air. Daylight found former biker-turned-Christian Big Jim Dunning sleeping comfortably in his portable tent. His last several months were a whirlwind of miracles, reconnecting with his father, and learning his old best friend was actually his brother. If that wasn't enough, to top it all off he learned he was also a father himself. That was more than a normal person could handle, but not Big Jim. He'd actually gotten a pretty good night's sleep camped out behind his grandmother Nanna's abandoned house in the back yard. Waking up to that old familiar smell of bacon was an unexpected bonus. When he would wake up to bacon as a youngster the smell of bacon always told him a special breakfast was waiting for him. Not long ago he woke up to the smell of bacon during one of his first encounters with his father after his return to town. The thought of that meeting on the mountain made him smile. His thoughts were starting to drift back to that day when the sharp snapping noise of a stick outside brought him back to reality.

"You awake in there?"

Big Jim instantly recognized the voice as belonging to his father.

"Yeah, I'm awake now, thanks to you! I'll be out as soon as I have a chance to freshen up."

The cheerful, joking tone of Big Jim's voice brought a big smile to the old man's face. After all the years of separation, every moment the two of the were together was precious to him and it always made him happy when things started off on a positive note.

"I think it's high time that we talk about what comes next for you," said the old man as Big Jim crawled out of the tent.

"Maybe, but I think it's high time we figured out what I should be calling you. Old man doesn't sound respectful, father sounds too formal. After all the time we've spent apart, I'm not sure dad feels right just yet."

"I answer to just about anything. That's not really important, but I've always been partial to Pop since that's what I called your granddad."

"Pop it is!"

"Okay, that's settled then. But that's not what I had in mind to talk about at all."

"What do you mean then? I don't get it."

"It's pretty simple. What do you plan on doing next with your life?"

"I hadn't really given it any thought."

"That's the problem."

"Problem?"

"Yes, problem. If you're just bouncing around like a cork in the ocean, it's hard to tell where you'll end up. You can't just keep sleeping in this old tent every night, and riding that beat-up old motorcycle all over the place with no direction, no place to go."

"My bike ain't beat up."

"You know what I mean. That's not the point I'm trying to make."

"What point are you trying to make?"

"What I'm trying to tell you is that it's time to leave your old life totally behind. You've had a big change in your life. I believe your life has a purpose and it's time to figure out what it is. It's time to be a productive part of society instead of a homeless guy on a motorcycle."

Big Jim laughed. "You're starting to sound just like the old guidance counselors back when I was in school. And I haven't had a home-type home since I left this place years ago."

"Well you do now. Provided you want it, that is."

"Say what?"

"I still hold the deed to this old house here. It's mine. Nanna left it to me when she passed. I'd like it if you and I could work together on it enough for you to live in it for a while. Me too, for that matter. It might be high time that I settle down too."

Jim paused at the thought and gazed at the house. It wasn't much to look at, definitely hadn't been lived in for a very long time, but it might be a pleasant change to have a roof over his head. It had been so long since he had a place to call home that the whole idea of it was foreign to him.

"I know what you're thinking," the old man continued, "but we wouldn't have to do it all at once. The old place is still pretty solid. We could board up all the busted windows, fix up the kitchen first, just start off with the necessities so we could live in it."

"You know, it really wouldn't take much for two old campers like us to make it livable."

"Yeah, I know. We're used to roughing it. This would be like living at the Hilton for us!"

With that thought in mind, Jim let his gaze go past his father and look at the old house in a different light. One could tell by the structure that it had been an upscale home at one time. There was a lot of fancy woodwork around the eaves of the second story, although it was obvious the paint had been worn off by the weather many years ago much like the rest of the house. Some of the windows still had a pane or two of glass left in them, but most of the windows had long since been broken out, probably by young kids just trying to see if they could hit a window with a rock.

"You really think we could make this a home?" He tried to keep the doubt out of his voice to please his father but Big Jim wasn't sure if he pulled it off.

"Well youngster, the big thing is making sure that roof didn't leak. Looks pretty good from out here, but we best go inside and check it out."

"Okay. Sounds like a plan."

The pair of them walked up to the rear of the house and cautiously climbed the steps on the back porch.

"Be careful on that first step Jimmy, it feels a little weak."

"Oh, I think I can take care of…….."

The step let out a crack that sounded like a rifle shot as it snapped in half under Big Jim's weight.

"You know, I told you to…."

"Yeah, I know," chuckled Big Jim as he pulled his right foot up out of the hole that was where the step used to be, "you told me to be careful."

"Well now that we've gotten that out of the way, come on up here."

"Find something interesting?"

"Not interesting, but encouraging. Looks to me like all these vines that grew up all over this porch actually protected the wood. It's in better shape up here than I imagined. If not for all the plants, the back porch might have been gone just like the front porch on this old house. Not only that, look at the windows. Looks like the kitchen windows might have been the only ones in the whole house to survive."

"Wow, that's quite a surprise," said Big Jim as he tried to look through a window, "but they're so dirty that maybe it's just all this dirt holding things together."

"Don't you worry, we'll get around to cleaning those windows. I have a feeling there are probably higher priorities inside waiting on us."

"You're probably right. How do we get in anyway? Go around the front and climb in one of the broken windows?"

The old man winked at him and pulled a key out of his pocket.

"For a long time I wondered if I would ever get a chance to use this key," said the old man as he put the key into the lock on the back door.

The key fit into the lock on the door, but it seemed like it might not be the right one. The old man couldn't get the lock to budge no matter how hard he tried. He wiggled, tugged, and shook the key up and down as hard as he could without having a result. Beads of sweat began to form on his brow from all the effort he was putting into this lock. He finally ran out of patience and stepped back away from the door to give up when the lock turned on its own before his eyes.

"Priority number one, get a new lock," said Big Jim laughing as he opened the door from the inside.

"But how…."

"You were so focused on getting that door open that you didn't notice me climbing in through the side window. At the rate you were going I figured it might be quicker."

"I should've known," said the old man shaking his head as he stepped inside.

Now that they were both inside, they looked around to see how much work lie ahead of them. Big Jim recognized the old wallpaper of Nanna's kitchen from when he was young. The rose print was now faded and falling off in some places, yet it still gave the old kitchen an elegant feel. The same old gas stove was still in place, but there was a big empty space where the refrigerator once was. The linoleum floor was different, but it was cracked and worn in numerous places. The old man ran his hands across the cabinets and smiled. At least they looked to still be in pretty good shape.

"I made these cabinets myself. It wasn't too long before you were born," said the old man wistfully.

"Wow. That's something I never knew. Looks like you're very talented."

"Thanks. It's just something that comes easy to me. A God-given talent if you will. I suspect you have one as well Jimmy."

"You think?"

"We've been apart for years. We've both been away from this town for years. Now we're not only back in town at the same time, we're back together as a family, not only you and me, but Brandon and your son Joshua too. The Lord works in mysterious ways and we've seen a lot of it here recently. I really believe you were brought back here for a purpose. If we can figure out how you're gifted, maybe we can get a clue what that purpose is."

"You're sounding like a cross between a prophet and a detective."

"Well, maybe we can crack this case and realize the prophecy while we work on this place together," laughed the old man.

"Maybe some of the other tenants can lend a hand too."

"Other tenants?"

"Yep."

Big Jim nodded towards the hallway. The old man turned to see a large, chubby squirrel enjoying a nut while listening to the conversation.

"Ah, a spy!" exclaimed the old man laughing.

"Oh, I don't know. By the way he's sitting there, I think he believes he owns the place."

"Could be, but if he doesn't pitch in and help, we'll have to give him the boot."

"Better run while you can little buddy," cackled Big Jim, "or you'll liable to end up as stew for supper!"

The squirrel dropped the nut and ran off as if he could understand every word.

"Well, it looks like a lot of work, but if this place is fit enough for squirrels to hole up in, I guess we could make it work for us. It will take a bit of cleaning up before we get started though."

"You're right there Jimmy. You know, this house is kind of like us. It's a mess inside, just like we were and our lives used to be. Then we let Jesus clean up all the junk and make us clean and whole. And that's just what we're going to do with this house."

"Yeah, I guess you're right about that."

"There's another thing that might be about the same. The Word says once we've cleaned ourselves up, we have to be careful or seven times as much junk will find its' way back into our lives. This house could be like that because if we don't fix the windows and doors, all kinds of stuff will come back in after we clean it out."

"I guess you're right about that too."

"Jimmy?"

"Yeah Pop?"

Being called Pop warmed the old man's heart and made him smile.

"Now that your spiritual house is cleaned up and you've given the keys to Jesus, the devil's going to come after you. Be careful and be on your guard all the time, okay?"

"Okay Pop, if you say so."

"I say so. The enemy is tricky, so you always have to watch out for an attack."

"You're probably right, but right now, I think maybe we better plan against an attack of squirrels. They might not like us moving into 'their' home."

"Probably so. We'll have to get some plastic and plywood to get this place a little more secure."

"Max might be able to tell us where there's a good place to pick that stuff up. I'll drop on over there and talk to him."

"You're right. Pastor Carson could probably point us in the right direction. I'm going to run up to Coal Creek and see if I can catch us a fish or two for lunch while you're doing that. We'll meet up here later."

"Sounds like a plan."

2
FINDING PURPOSE

Big Jim could see Pastor Max Carson's little girl Mary happily playing out back as he approached Max's house. It still amazed Big Jim every time he thought about when he and Mary first met. He was about as mean-looking and scary as they come, yet Mary wasn't afraid and treated him as a friend right from the beginning.

"Mister Jim! Mister Jim!" squealed Mary as she ran up to give Big Jim a hug.

"How's my favorite girl?" asked Big Jim as he lifted Mary high up into the air, "Is your daddy home?"

"He sure is Mister Jim, I'll take you to him."

It was a curious picture, the little girl leading the big guy by the hand towards the house, but if anyone were watching it would be obvious that this unlikely pair truly adored each other. At least it was obvious to Mary's mother, Emma, as she watched the pair through the kitchen window and smiled at them.

"Daddy, Daddy, Mister Jim's here to see you!" called out Mary as they approached the door to Pastor Max Carson's office.

Max just shook his head and smiled as he opened the door to find Big Jim twirling Mary around through the air like a little doll.

"Hey Jim, how's it going?"

"Not bad, buddy. I came to get a little information from you."

"No problem. Come on in and grab a seat and make yourself comfortable. Mary, you can go play while Jim and I visit, okay?"

"Okay daddy. Mister Jim, will you come to my tea party after you're done visiting with daddy?"

"We'll see, Mary, we'll see."

"Okay Mister Jim, I'll set a place for you," said Mary as she happily skipped away.

"That's quite a kid you got there Max."

Max laughed. "We like her. Now what can I do for you?"

"Pop and I are going to fix up Nanna's old house and stay in it. We thought you might be able to tell us where we could get some supplies cheap."

"Pop?"

"Yeah, now that we're together again, I wanted to call him something besides 'old man.' That's what we came up with."

"Well it's about time. You guys have been apart for so many years you shouldn't be wasting any time being a family again. What about Brandon?"

"We haven't told him about it yet. He'd be welcome to join us, but I imagine he'll keep staying with his mom. After all, we haven't been brothers for that long you know."

"The way I remember it, you guys were brothers whether you knew it or not back in the old days," laughed Max, "so much has changed in these last few months. It's really been a whirlwind for you."

"You got that right. I went from having no one to having a father, a brother," big Jim paused, getting a little teary-eyed at the memory, "and a son."

"We can't forget your second birth either."

"No we can't. That Jesus dude changed my life. I would never have believed such blessings could be possible."

"It has been amazing watching the miracles surrounding Brandon's healing. Your transformation has been pretty miraculous in itself."

"I'm a new man Max. The old Jim is gone."

"Keep your guard up and keep following Jesus, Jim. We don't want the old evil coming back and bringing friends along."

"Funny you should say that Max. Pop was just saying about the same thing. Something about the house being clean."

"Yes, that's in the book of Luke, Jim. It talks about evil spirits coming back to where they came from and bringing seven even more evil spirits with them. You end up in even worse shape than when you started that way."

"I don't think the world could survive with me being seven times worse than what I was when I came here. I thank God every day that you were here to help me Max."

"Well, at least you're giving credit where it's due. You're the one that followed the Holy Spirit, I was just along for the ride."

"And what a ride it was!"

"Jim, I don't think the ride's over yet. I think there's more to come."

"Could be. Pop said something about me finding my purpose too. Maybe that will be part of the ride."

"Well you can't run around on that old bike and sleep in that ragged, old tent forever, you know."

"Wow. Déjà vu. That's almost the exact same thing Pop said."

"Really? Might be the Spirit at work here."

"You think so? After all we've been through and seen in the last few months, it's hard to imagine even more."

"When the Lord's involved, anything is possible."

"So true. Anyway, what about those supplies? Do you know where we can get some stuff? I need to keep moving along here because I have a tea date outside waiting on me."

"It's always amazed me how Mary looked past your rough exterior to see you for yourself. Just about everyone else was scared to death of you at first."

"She's an amazing little girl Max. You should be proud."

"I am Jim. I am. I'm proud of Joshua too."

"Max, I can never thank you enough for raising my son so well."

"He was never a problem, Jim. It seemed like there was always a special blessing on him."

"Something else I can never give enough thanks for."

"Give thanks to where it's due, Jim. This whole thing of us all coming together has been quite a miracle."

"It hasn't been that many months ago that I would've told you I'd never give God credit for anything, and now I just can't get over how good God has been to me. It's like my eyes have been opened up to a whole new world."

"Just watch your back Jim. When you least expect it, the evil one will try and steal some of that glory God's given you away."

"You and Pop been talking behind my back? You keep saying about the same things he did this morning."

"Really? Maybe the Spirit's trying to tell you something Jim."

"Could be. Right now, let's get back to what I came here for. Do you know where we can get some supplies?"

Max laughed. "I guess we did get off the track a little bit didn't we? There's a guy in my congregation named Kevin Wilson. He lives over on the other side of town beside where the old softball field used to be. Remember where that is?"

"Yeah, I remember. I remember how bad we used to make fun of you because you'd swing the bat like a girl and most of the girls could hit better than you too."

Big Jim gave Max a playful poke in the arm so he'd know he was just kidding him.

"You just had to bring those memories up, didn't you?"

"One of the few things I remember from school was being told that if you didn't learn your history, you'd have to live it all over again."

"You should remember that. It seems like the teacher told you that every day in history class because you never paid attention."

"You had to bring THAT up didn't you?"

Max poked Big Jim back and started laughing.

"Anyway, Jim, Kevin lives in the green house by the ball field. You can't miss it because there's nothing else over there anymore. He has his own construction company and might be able to help you out with some supplies."

"Great, I'll run over there and see what he's got as soon as I take care of this tea date I got waiting for me outside. Thanks Max!"

"Don't mention it Jim. Let me know how you make out."

"Sure thing. Later dude!"

3
A GIFT REVEALED

"Max hit the nail on the head," thought Big Jim to himself as he pulled in Kevin Wilson's driveway, "no other houses around here, let alone green ones.

Big Jim slowly brought his motorcycle to a stop. Before he shut it off, he could see a man out behind the house working so intently on something that he didn't even seem to notice Big Jim's arrival. Big Jim kept his eyes on the man while he shut off his engine, set the motorcycle up on the kickstand, and dismounted. Still no reaction of any kind. Whatever it was the man was working on had his undivided attention.

"Uh...Mr. Wilson?"

Big Jim made sure to call out to the man before getting any closer. He knew he was scary enough as it was without sneaking up on someone.

"That's me," the man replied, never looking up from his task.

"I was told you might be able to help me out," said Big Jim as he walked towards Mr. Wilson.

"Oh really? And who might have told you such thing?"

"My buddy, Pastor Max Carson."

Kevin Wilson looked up and literally jumped at the sudden sight of the big man before him. He definitely was expecting to look up and find a normal looking person and Big Jim was anything but normal. He pondered Big Jim's statement a bit, taking the time to look him over and consider his own personal safety while he thought about it.

"I know Max. I go to his church when I can make it. You must be Jim Dunning. I've heard about you."

"Yes sir, that's me. I hope you've only heard good things," said Big Jim laughing.

"Let's just say I've heard things and leave it at that," Kevin said with a chuckle, "now what is it that I can help you with?"

"Well, my father and I are going to start working on our house and we'll need some stuff to close up the broken out windows and doors to start with. I should mention that we don't have much money to work with either."

"Lack of funds always presents a problem."

Kevin went back to what he was doing, which Jim could now see was pulling on a starter cord to try and start a small engine mounted on a small piece of machinery. Jim could also see that he wasn't having much luck.

"Air."

"I'm sorry, what did you say?" asked Kevin as he continued pulling the cord with no results.

"Air."

"Air?"

"Yes, air. Your engine isn't starting because it's not getting any air."

"You think so? How can you tell that just from standing there?"

"Well, it just sounds to me like it's not getting air. Let me have a look at it."

Kevin stepped aside so Big Jim could go to work. It hardly took any time at all for him to twist off the thumb screw that held the cover on the machine's air filter. A second thumb screw held the air filter in place and Big Jim removed that with equal speed and held the air filter up for Kevin to see.

"It's pretty much what I thought. Your air filter is so full of dirt and crud the engine couldn't breathe."

Kevin stood staring at the dirty filter dumb-founded.

"Got a clean shop rag?"

Kevin pulled a shop rag from his rear pocket and handed it to Big Jim. He watched with curiosity as Big Jim carefully inspected and wiped all the dirt and grime away from the area the air filter came from and knocked as much dirt out of the filter as he could. When it was clean enough for Jim's satisfaction, he put it all back together and gave the starter cord a good pull. The engine sputtered a little, but still didn't start.

"Got a spark plug socket and a ratchet?"

Kevin motioned to a tool box sitting on the back of his truck. Big Jim opened it up and quickly found what he was looking for. He removed the spark plug, and cleaned it off with the shop rag too. He did a few more things that Kevin didn't understand and put the spark plug back in. This time when he pulled the starter cord, the engine roared to life on the first pull. After he was satisfied that it was running smoothly, Big Jim shut the engine off.

"There you go. I suggest you don't run it any more until you get a new air filter to put on there. It will just suck dirt into the engine otherwise and we don't want that."

"Amazing. Simply amazing."

"What is?"

"It's amazing that you knew just what to do when all you did was listen to me trying to start that thing."

Big Jim just shrugged his shoulders.

"I've done the same thing a bunch of times. It's no big deal. I just seem to know what the problem is after a little thought and investigation."

"You, sir, have a gift. That's all there is to it. You know, it was going to cost me a bit of time and good money to get this thing fixed, so maybe we can work out a deal here. For what you've done for me, I can let you have some plastic and scrap pieces of plywood for your project."

Big Jim smiled and mouthed a silent "thank you" heavenward.

"That would be great. We really appreciate your help. Thank you very much!"

"No, it's me that should be thanking you. I would've been in a world of hurt tomorrow without that thing running and you bailed me out."

"Well I'm glad I could help you. What is that thing anyway?"

"It's a float machine used to smooth concrete floors off. I have a floor for an important client to do tomorrow and he's not the kind that would be too understanding if he had to wait for this machine to get fixed."

"That sounds interesting. Do you need any help? I should probably be looking for some sort of job so there'll be money to buy other supplies as we need them."

"Well, I don't really need any extra help on this project. I'm just a small time operator and mostly work by myself. Have you done a lot of construction work before?"

"Well, to be honest, I've not done any yet. Working on our house will be my first experience."

"That's too bad. Usually when I do need help, I need someone with experience. Say, do you live nearby? If you're not too far away, we can load up the scrap plywood on my truck and I'll deliver it for you."

"That would be great. I don't think I'd have much luck carrying plywood on my bike."

"Bike?"

"Yeah, I came here on my motorcycle."

Kevin looked surprised to see a motorcycle sitting in the driveway.

"I guess I was trying so hard to get this thing running, I never noticed you showing up. Looks like a mighty fine bike from here."

Kevin walked over to Big Jim's motorcycle appearing to be interested. Big Jim followed along behind waiting to see what Kevin was up to. When they got to it, Kevin kneeled down to take a close look at the engine. He walked around the motorcycle twice, pausing to look at each part from several different angles, sometimes seeming to nod with approval.

"You take care of this thing yourself?"

"Yes sir. That bike and I have been through a lot together."

"It's pretty old, so I know you didn't buy it new. Did you get it from the original owner?"

"Well, Mr. Wilson, to be honest, I never knew who owned most of it. I put it together mostly from junk parts and other pieces that people gave me. It's hard to tell how many bikes it took to make this one."

"Amazing. You have to be some sort of mechanical genius to do that and end up with something that looks this good. That gives me an idea. I think I may know where you can earn a few dollars. It won't make you rich, but I think I know a fellow that has more of this kind of work than he can handle and he may be willing to pay you to help out."

"That would be wonderful! Thank you very much! Where can I find this guy?"

"He owns and operates Miner's Hardware over in Coalburg. That's only a few miles from here. He repairs a lot of lawn mowers, four-wheelers, and that kind of thing besides running the store. Last time I was over there, his workshop was overflowing and lawn mowers were sitting all over the place outside. Might be a situation made to order for you."

"Sounds like God's provision to me. I'll check it out after we get these supplies squared away."

4
BOB

It was an easy ride to Coalburg, only a few miles in fact. The narrow, twisting road was actually a pleasure to run a motorcycle on and Big Jim loved every minute of it. He had forgotten how beautiful the forest was along the road, every turn revealed scenery that looked like it belonged on a post card. It had been a long, long time since he felt this kind of exhilaration on the open road. The change in his life since he became born again really gave him a new appreciation for just about everything. Along the last straight stretch of road leading into Coalburg were the old coke ovens that fascinated him as a child. There were a lot of relics of the old glory days of the coal industry along the road sides near all the small towns in the area, but these ovens always drew his attention more than anything else. At some point during all the years he was gone, someone had gone to the trouble of restoring the ovens and it looked just like they were good as new, just waiting to produce a fresh batch of coke. What had once been a row of ugly, broken holes in the ground had been transformed into a fresh piece of scenery. He couldn't help but think that his own transformation wasn't all that different from those old coke ovens. He had gone from being ugly and broken down spiritually to being transformed into a new creature. That thought had put a big smile on Big Jim's face as he pulled up to Miner's Hardware Store. Like all the other small towns around, Coalburg had once been a bustling little coal-mining town years ago, thriving and full of stores, but now that the coal industry was long gone, there wasn't much going in the town. Just like those old coke ovens, Miner's Hardware Store was one of the reminders around the area of what had once been. It was hard to tell just how old the building was, but it was plain to see that it had been around for a long time. Somewhere in his memory he thought he had heard somewhere that this was the old company store for the local coal mines, and it looked every bit the part from the outside. The large display windows in the front were definitely from a time long gone by. The wooden trim work was far more detailed than anything modern and appeared to have gotten a fresh coat of paint in the not too distant past. The brick work was definitely old, but it appeared to have been well taken care of too. One of the windows had a display of old mining equipment and the other had a display of the latest hunting clothes. The wooden steps up to the front door made those old, familiar creaking noises just like all the stores around town did when he was a kid. A sign in the front door proudly proclaimed "IF WE DON'T HAVE IT, YOU DON'T NEED IT." The only thing that told him for sure he was still in the right century was the eye-catching sticker on the door warning robbers of the electronic surveillance system. As he opened the door, an old-time bell announced his presence to anyone inside. Looking around he could see that the sign in the door may not have been an idle boast. There was indeed a vast assortment of just about everything imaginable in this store. Large bins full of a large variety of nails were off to his right, followed by an assortment of nuts, bolts, and other fasteners. Off to his left was a large selection of household goods and cleaning supplies. Behind that appeared to be a display of gardening tools.

"Can I help you find something young man?"

Big Jim was so focused on taking in all the different merchandise in the store that he failed to notice the lady who must have popped up from behind the counter where they made keys. She was very short, so she could've easily been hidden in one of the aisles too. She had a cheery, grandmotherly look about her that immediately made him feel welcome to be there.

"Well yes, yes you can. I'm looking for the guy that owns this place. I need to talk to him about something."

"You'll be able to find him towards the back of the store. I last saw him in the paint section. He may still be there."

"Thank you, ma'am, that's a big help."

"Thank you for coming into our store today," said the woman in a still cheery voice.

Big Jim was still amazed at all the different things packed into this little store as he started toward the back. There was a Plumbing section, Electrical section, Welding section, Tools section, and a Paint section all in the path he was walking. He saw a man back in the paint section just as the lady had told him so he hurried back to make sure he didn't lose sight of him. The man was stacking up cans of paint on a shelf and didn't notice Jim approaching. Jim was about to say something when a memory clicked in his brain. He knew this man. At least he thought he did. It had been a long time, but he was pretty sure it was his old shop teacher from high school.

"Uh, Mr. Korreck?"

The man turned to face Big Jim.

"Mr. Korreck is my father. He's been living in Heaven for a long time so he's not here. Call me Bob."

"That just doesn't feel right Mr. Korreck."

"Bob."

"If you say so Mr. Kor....I mean, Bob."

"That's better. Now what can I do for you young man?"

"You don't recognize me do you?"

"Son, a lot of people show up in this store, but I've never seen anyone that looked even remotely like you, and I think I'd remember if I did."

"You are the Mr. Korreck that taught shop class aren't you?"

"That was a long time ago. Now I'm just Bob."

"Well, you haven't seen me for a very long time."

"That explains that. Now who are you?"

"Jim Dunning."

Bob paused to look Jim over a bit. He took a step back and then looked some more.

"Dunning, eh? You've changed a bit."

"It has been awhile you know. You don't look any different."

"Flattery will get you nowhere son. It looks to me like it's been awhile since your last haircut and beard trim too."

Big Jim stroked his beard.

"Well, I guess it has been awhile. I hadn't really given it much thought to tell you the truth."

"Obviously. Now, Jim Dunning, what is it you want?"

"I heard you might have some work here I could do."

"Someone told you wrong. I'm a small-time operator here. I can't afford to hire anyone else."

"That's not what I meant, sir. I was talking to Kevin Wilson, and he told me you might need help with some engine work."

"I know Mr. Wilson. Has a small construction business over in Brooksville. Why would he be talking to you?"

"Well sir, my friend, Pastor Max Carson, told me Kevin might be able to help me with some construction supplies so I went to see him."

"Don't know the Carson fellow, really. I do remember having him in school though. Good kid. Always worked hard. Trustworthy. You, on the other hand, were a totally different story."

"I know. You're right. And I apologize for anything wrong I did back then. I'm not the same person as I was when I was younger."

"Oh really? Why should I believe that?"

"To be honest, I can't really give you a reason. Just give me a chance, that's all I ask. If you have some engine work, let me help with that and you can pay me what you want and only for what I do. I just need to make a little bit of money right now, I'm not asking for a full-time job."

"Just what do you need that 'little bit of money' for? Drugs? Alcohol?"

Jim's temper was beginning to rise up just a bit. Controlling his anger was something he was working on, but he wasn't expecting a cross examination like this, let alone from his old teacher Mr. Korreck. Mr. Korreck had been the sternest teacher by far in Big Jim's life. He always demanded the most from his class, yet they all respected him not only because he demanded the respect, but because he returned that respect to them when they acted properly. It was only the memory of their past history and the working of the Spirit within him that allowed Big Jim to remain calm.

"Aren't you being a little harsh, Mr. Korreck?"

"Bob."

Big Jim closed his eyes and shook his head.

"Okay, 'Bob' why are you being so hard on me?"

"Don't you remember Mr. Dunning, I was hard on you back in school too."

"You were hard on everyone."

"True. But I was a bit harder on you than I was on your classmates."

"School wasn't a happy time for me, so I try to forget as much as I can, but why were you so hard on me then?"

"Because I saw something in you, Mr. Dunning. I saw potential that had a good chance of not being reached. I wanted you to see that potential and make something of yourself. I failed in doing that and that means I failed you. I'm sorry."

Big Jim wasn't sure, but it looked like tears were starting to form in Mr. Korreck's eyes. When he was young, he couldn't have imagined that being possible.

"Mr. Korreck, I'll admit I made a wreck of my life, but there was nothing you could've done about any of it. I'm a different guy now, I'm not the same."

"What do you mean you're not the same?"

"I know Jesus now. I'm trying to follow him."

Bob looked at Jim thoughtfully for a second.

"Come with me."

Bob led Big Jim out the back door of the store, past small buildings where lumber and bags of concrete were stored to a cement block building at the back of the lot. Once there, he stooped over to open up a large garage door on the side of the building. Inside it seemed like every inch of the building was filled with lawn mowers, chain saws, four-wheelers, motorcycles, scooters, and just about anything else imaginable that had an engine on it.

"As you can see, I'm a little behind here. I'll tell you what. If you want to give this a shot, I'm willing to give you a chance. Come back tomorrow and I'll let you try fixing one of these on a trial basis. If that works out, we'll talk."

"It's a deal, Mr. Korreck. What time do you want me to be here?"

"Bob."

Big Jim let out a big laugh.

"Okay, it's a deal, 'Bob'."

"I open at 8 o'clock in the morning. Any time between 8 and 9 will be fine."

"Great! I'll be here. One more thing Bob."

"Yes?"

"Call me Jim."

Now it was Bob's turn to laugh.

"Okay Jim. See you tomorrow."

The two men shook hands to seal their deal and walked back through the store.

"Bernice?" Bob called out, "where are you?"

"Over here Bob, putting the kerosene heater parts away."

Big Jim now understood that Bernice was the older lady that had helped him in the store. Bob led Jim over to where they heard Bernice call out from.

"Bernice, this is Jim Dunning, Jim, this is Bernice Decker, my helper. Bernice, Jim is going to be doing some work for me tomorrow, so if you're here before me, it's okay to let him in."

"Sure thing, Bob. Pleased to meet you Mr. Dunning," Bernice said as she stuck out her hand to shake Jim's.

"Jim. Pleased to meet you too, Bernice."

Big Jim shot a quick wink in Bob's direction to let him know the impersonation of him was intentional. Bob picked up that Jim impersonated him during the introduction and winked back.

"Well, Bob, now that all the pleasantries are out of the way, I must be going. I have a lot of work to do back home."

"You just make sure you're ready to work when you show up tomorrow."

Bob's voice carried that stern teacher tone of old.

"Yes sir, Mr. Korreck!"

"Bob."

They were both laughing pretty hard as Big Jim went out the door. Bernice just looked at the two of them with a puzzled look. Bob was just finishing up his laughing spell when a screechy-sounding voice called out from the end of the aisle.

"Mr. Korreck?"

Bob turned around to find himself face-to-face with Margaret Messner, wife of Pastor Herbert Messner from the Brethren Friendship church over in Brooksville.

"Yes, ma'am?"

"Did I hear you correctly? Were you saying that man will be working here?"

"Yes ma'am, you did."

"Mr. Korreck, I shop here because it's an upstanding family establishment. If people like that start to work here, I shall take my business elsewhere."

"People like what?"

"Like that big, ugly bully. That long, scraggily hair and beard are such a disgrace! Those biker clothes are an embarrassment too. Mark my words, you make that man welcome here in this town and soon we'll be surrounded with undesirable people like that. It won't even be safe to go out in the street anymore!"

The way her voice raised in volume and intensity, Bob was sure she was about to pop a cork.

"Well ma'am, I'm sure sorry you feel that way," said Bob in the politest voice he could muster.

"Are you saying you're going to let him work here after all?"

"If he proves he can do the job, yes. I'm sorry if that offends you, but the way I see it, it's really none of your business who I hire to work here. It's my business and it's my choice."

"Well then, it's my choice to go elsewhere. And I'll be telling everyone I know not to shop here too."

"Thank you for your concern ma'am and have a nice day."

Bernice had to turn her head so Mrs. Messner couldn't see her laughing at Bob's trumped up show of false courtesy. Mrs. Messner just glared at Bob, turned and slammed the door behind her as she left the store.

"Do you think she'll cause trouble, Bob?" asked Bernice.

"It would appear she's going to do her best to. It's still none of her business."

5
AROUND THE TABLE

When Big Jim pulled into the driveway at the old house he thought he'd be finding it completely dark, but it was just late enough in the evening for him to see a light shining from the kitchen window. Definitely signs of life there. After he parked the bike and shut down the engine, the sounds of laughter also told him that he'd be finding more than just his father inside. Sure enough, as he walked along the house he could see through the kitchen window that his brother, Brandon, and his son, Joshua were there along with his father. Seeing them all together made him pause to think of the series of miracles that reunited this improbable family. It had to be God's hand that brought him back to Brooksville the same way his father had been led to return. To have that miracle topped by learning that his best childhood friend Brandon was actually his half-brother and then be able to donate his bone marrow to save him just in time was beyond incredible. All that and then to learn that he had a son, Joshua, that he didn't even know existed was about enough to make him explode with happiness. How thankful he was that Pastor Max had raised Joshua to be such a fine, young man! The sudden rush of appreciation brought Big Jim to his knees in a prayer of thanks for all that God had done for him. He hadn't prayed for very long when he realized the sounds coming from the house had stopped. Slowly opening his eyes, he looked up and saw all of them looking down at him smiling. Brandon waved at him to come inside. Jim got up, wiped the dirt from his knees and went to the back door. He couldn't help but notice the step he had broken earlier in the day had been repaired as he made his way to the back door. His eyes were upon the new lock on the rear door when Brandon opened the door before him.

"Get in here before you scare all the night critters away, buddy," said Brandon.

"Well, I figure you probably took care of all that when you showed up here," replied Big Jim laughing.

Big Jim went inside and surveyed the scene. It looked like the trio had made a lot of progress while he was gone. The light that he noticed from the outside was a lantern burning on a table. That light revealed that the room had been cleaned up and sealed off from the outside. The biggest surprise was the old stove. Not only was it functioning, but there was a large skillet full of fresh trout frying on top.

"Wow, it sure looks like someone was busy this afternoon."

"Yeah," said Pop Dunning, "Joshua and Brandon really helped a lot. Brandon found that old table upstairs and we brought it down. Those chairs around it aren't much to look at, but they'll hold us up. Max was able to hook up the stove for us too!"

"And the fish?"

"Well, the Lord blessed me with a bountiful catch over at Coal Creek. Brandon and Joshua brought over the skillet and a few plates and utensils so we could eat it here. Pretty snazzy, eh?"

"Yep, we're living in style!"

Brandon laughed, "now if we could only figure out a way to make you stylish Big Ugly, we'd really be accomplishing something!"

"Ugly? The only thing you've got going for you is my bone marrow."

"Well, my brother, you have no idea how hard it is to make that ugly marrow look good."

The pair's playful exchange was interrupted by the sound of Joshua and Pop Dunning's laughter.

"You guys are just too, too much," laughed Joshua.

"Definitely two of a kind," chuckled Pop Dunning.

"Oh, pipe down, you two," laughed Big Jim, "how about we do something about those fish? They're starting to look pretty good!"

"Right you are Jimmy! You young pups grab some plates and forks and take a seat around the table. I'll serve up the fish!" said Pop Dunning.

"You don't have to tell me twice!" exclaimed Brandon eagerly.

The three of them sat around the makeshift dining table eyeing up the fresh fish like they hadn't eaten in months as Pop Dunning placed it on their plates. They all wanted to start eating immediately, but out of respect for Pop, they waited until he was sitting there with them.

"The Lord has provided us with a meal fit for kings, youngsters. Good food and family all in one place. We are truly blessed."

The others could see a small tear forming in the corner of Pop's eye, but didn't want to mention it because not only were they were all feeling how special the moment was, they were also afraid of breaking down in tears themselves. Tough guys weren't supposed to cry, right? Joshua, the youngest could sense what was going on and broke the silence.

"Guys, I think we need to give thanks. I'll say the blessing for this meal."

The other three nodded in agreement and bowed their heads.

"Father, we give you thanks and praise for this food you've provided us here tonight. I also thank you for bringing us all together here. After so much in the world conspired to keep us apart, it was your plan and your strength that brought us all together as a family in a way only you could've done. We're humbled by what you've done for us Father and we ask that you keep watching over us, keeping us safe, healthy, and following you. We ask this in Jesus' name, amen."

The prayer had touched them all and they were all quiet for a time, afraid to be the first one to speak, afraid to show how much they were caught up in the unbelievable series of miracles that had brought their lives together at this point. Once again, it was Joshua who had to break the silence.

"I love you guys. Now let's dig in!"

"Yeah, me too. I couldn't have said it better," said Big Jim.

"Words of wisdom, kiddo, words of wisdom," said Brandon.

Pop Dunning was too choked up to speak so he just shook his head and took a bite of fish.

"Great fish Pop, the best I've had in a long, long time," said Big Jim.

"Wait a minute. 'Pop'?" asked Brandon, looking back and forth at Big Jim and Pop Dunning.

"Yeah, Pop," said Big Jim, "we decided earlier today that I should be calling him something other than 'old man' and that's what we came up with."

"Well it does have a ring to it," said Brandon, "is it okay if I call you 'Pop' too? I'm a part of this family too, you know."

"Well," said Pop Dunning laughing, "I guess it's only right that my sons call me the same thing."

"What about me? I need to call you something too," said Joshua.

"Well, what about 'Pap'?"

"Sure thing Pap!"

Joshua turned to Big Jim. "What should I be calling you now?"

Jim paused and then hung his head.

"I don't know. I may be your father, but I don't deserve being called 'Dad' or 'Pop' or anything else like that. Max deserves all the credit for who you are today. If you knew some of what I've done, you probably wouldn't want to be here in this room right now."

"It wasn't an accident that God brought you back here to me. I don't care what you've done or who you were, and God doesn't either. You've asked for forgiveness so whatever you've done has been cast into the sea of forgiveness. I forgive you too. You're my father."

"I know everything you're saying is true, but my dreams have been haunting me. They keep reminding me of the bad things I've done. I don't think I deserve having a son like you."

"And Jesus didn't deserve to endure all the pain he did to cover our sins. He loves us. He loves you. I love you and these other guys too. You didn't need to do anything to deserve it."

Jim paused, thinking over what Joshua had said.

"I still have trouble understanding all this Jesus stuff sometimes, but I believe what you're saying. Still, I don't deserve anything special. How about you just call me 'Jim' for now?"

"Okay, if that's what you want. You're selling yourself short though. You're a changed man, you're not who you used to be."

"I know. I know. I'm still learning and growing every day."

"Speaking of growing, how did that job lead you had work out?" asked Pop Dunning.

"Great," said Big Jim, "I landed a part-time job doing some small engine work."

"That's great Jimbo!" exclaimed Brandon, "you always had a certain touch with any engine you messed with. Even way back in high school you could work magic with an engine."

"Funny you should mention high school. I'm actually going to work for our old shop teacher, Mr. Korreck."

"Mr. Korreck? I heard that he bought a store somewhere, but I never really cared enough to find out where."

"He has Miner's Hardware, over in Coalburg. Looked like he had a good bit of work for me to do."

"Jimmy, that's God's provision," said Pop Dunning, "He's going to take good care of us and provide for us so we can make this place livable again."

"Livable? This place is already like the Taj Mahal compared to my old tent. Looks like there's enough room in here that we could put our sleeping bags down and make this our bedroom too!"

"Slow down youngster, I think I'll stick to the comfort of my camper for the time being. You can have this room to yourself. If you need company, that squirrel we saw earlier is probably still around."

"We'll give that squirrel a free ride for a little while longer since he was here before us, but at some point, he'll have to leave or become supper."

"I'd stick around here with you, Big Ugly, but I have this thing they call a bed that I've really grown accustomed to. You'll have to ugly up the place yourself," said Brandon laughing.

"I'll stay here with you Jim," said Joshua, "I'd like to spend more time with you."

"That would be great Joshua, but you have a home to get back to. You belong there, not camping out in the kitchen of an old house."

"I belong here with you Jim."

"You belong at home with your mama and the dad that raised you Joshua. Not with a dumb, ugly guy that's still trying to figure out what he's doing. It's for your own good."

It was obvious that Joshua wasn't happy with Big Jim's decision, but he wasn't going to argue.

"I guess I better be going then," said Joshua, his voice shaking a little.

"Not till you clean up your plate, young man," said Pop Dunning with a laugh. He could sense the disappointment in Joshua's voice and was trying to lighten the mood.

"Aw, leave him alone, I can take care of that leftover fish," said Brandon with a laugh, also trying to lighten things up a bit.

"Alright. You guys win. I'll finish my fish."

Big Jim just sat silently through the rest of the meal, wondering how the mood of the evening had changed so fast. The look on Joshua's face was something he'd never seen out of him before. The feeling of concern he had because of that look was something new for him too.

6
THE THREAT

The bad feelings from the night before were still stinging Big Jim's heart as he rode towards his new job in Coalburg. The feeling was very different from what he'd felt after all the good times and miracles of the last several months, but it didn't take long for him to remember this feeling from all the bad times in the past. Maybe he should've just let Joshua spend the night and avoid the conflict. Part of him felt like he let him down, but deep down he knew he was afraid. Afraid that Joshua would turn into what he used to be if they spent too much time together. He was so wrapped up in his emotions that he pulled up in front of Miner's Hardware store without remembering any of the ride.

"Maybe an honest day's work will help me take my mind off of all this," Big Jim thought to himself as he walked up the steps to the front door. The door was open, so he walked on in.

"Anybody home?"

"Back here, Jim."

Jim walked back the row of garden tools to where he thought he heard Bernice's voice coming from. It appeared that she was putting away large bags of dog food when he found her.

"Good morning, Bernice. Is Mr. Korreck around here anywhere?"

"I think he's out back getting some jobs lined up for you to do," she said as she waved her hand towards the back door. "And don't forget to call him Bob."

That made Big Jim laugh.

"Sure thing Bernice."

"Jim, just call me Bernie, it rolls off the tongue easier."

"Will you correct me if I get it wrong, like Mr. Korreck does?"

"Maybe, maybe not. I guess we'll see won't we?" Bernice said with a wink.

"I guess we will. Thanks….um….Bernie."

Bernice laughed, "you're quite welcome, Mr. Dunning."

"Jim."

They were both laughing as Big Jim went out the back door. Right away he could hear metallic sounds coming from the rear of the lot so he knew Bob was back there as Bernice had thought. The metallic sounds grew louder as Jim got closer and he could soon see Bob wrestling with a large lawn mower.

"Hey, do you need any help with that?" Jim called out.

Bob replied with a laugh, "No, but you might."

"I take it that's my first job?"

"You take it right. This is old John Higby's riding tractor. I think it's been here longer than the rest of this junk, so you'll start with it."

"Any idea of what's wrong?"

"Yes. It doesn't work."

"Well, thanks for the diagnosis, Mr. Obvious," laughed Jim.

"You asked. I told you."

"I expected a little more information than that."

"I just passed on what I was told when he dropped it off."

"I guess my work's cut out for me then."

"It certainly is. If you can't hack it, you can get your jacket."

"I remember you using that old phrase back in school."

"Well, it still fits. If you can handle this one, you should be able to handle the rest. Let's see what you've got. If you get that one figured out, you can move on to those over there." Bob waved his hand towards a line of at least six more lawn tractors at the other end of the building.

"No problem sir, no problem. You do have tools here, don't you?"

"Yes, they're in the big cabinet inside. And don't call me sir, I haven't been knighted just yet."

"It's a shame. Sir Bob has a nice ring to it."

"Cut it out and get to work. It's time for me to get back to the store and make some money. It's time for you to make some money for me too."

Big Jim surveyed the lawn tractor before him as Bob was walking back to the store. It didn't appear to be beat up any, but just by looking at it he could tell it never had any sort of regular maintenance. It was covered by so much dirt it was hard to even tell what color it was.

"Well," he thought to himself, "I guess the first thing to do is check the engine out. Looks like there's gas in the tank, oil on the dipstick." Big Jim gave the engine a spin by hand to make sure it wasn't locked up and then turned the ignition switch. Nothing. It was time to check out the tools and dig deeper into the mower to figure out this puzzle.

As Big Jim was starting to face the challenge of the lawn mower, another challenge was unfolding inside the store. Bernice had seen Mrs. Messner climbing the front steps of the store and rushed to open the door for her. Mrs. Messner had a very sour look on her face before she even got to the door and Bernice was going to try her best to make Mrs. Messner happy as soon as she set foot in the door. It was a losing battle right from the start.

"Bernice!"

"Yes Mrs. Messner?"

"Where's Korreck? I want to talk to him right now!"

"He's out back, Mrs. Messner. If you'll just be patient I'm sure…"

"I will not be patient, I demand to see him right now!" The tone of her voice was quite unsettling.

Bob could hear the commotion as soon as he stepped in the back door. He had a suspicion something like this might happen. He sighed to himself and started towards the front of the store. He never had a problem speaking his mind, but he always hated dealing with people who thought they knew better than him what should be on his mind.

"Hello, Margaret, what can I do for you?" Bob put forth his sweetest voice, hoping that would calm her down a little.

"Mr. Korreck! I warned you about hiring undesirables to work here and it looks like you didn't listen to me. I saw that beast's motorcycle parked alongside your store and decided I had better take care of this situation. Did you go ahead and give that animal a job?"

"Yes ma'am. I'm trying him out to see if he knows what he's doing first, but I expect him to do fine."

"Fine? Fine? What of our nice little towns? What of our children? We'll be overrun by dirty bikers, probably all drinking, doing drugs, and who knows what else? We can't have that sort of criminal element around here!"

"Ma'am, it's just my opinion, but shouldn't we presume him to be innocent until proven guilty of…now just what crime was it you're trying to hang him with?"

"Don't you smart mouth me, Mr. Korreck! That…that man is no more than an animal. You can tell that just by the way he looks. I bet he already has cased your store and you'll find it empty of anything valuable by tomorrow morning. You can't trust that type!"

"Type? What type would that be?"

"The type that's not decent folk like us."

"So you're measuring him by your own yardstick then?"

"Don't get smart with me, Korreck. I know my rights. Either you fire him right now, or I'm going to march out of here and tell everyone to take their business elsewhere. And keep their doors locked and ready to call 9-1-1 when that animal is on the loose."

Bob walked over to the door and held it open.

"I'm sorry you feel that way Margaret. But as long as 'that animal,' as you call him, is doing a competent job and there is work for him to do, I'll be giving him a paycheck. Good day, Mrs. Messner."

"Fine, Mr. Korreck. We'll have to do it your way. I'll go out and make sure there won't be any work for him to do, then. I'll tell everyone that you're in cahoots with the devil and you hire evil people to work here. Good bye."

Margaret Messner was so angry Bob and Bernice could practically hear her feet stomping the whole way back to her car. They just stood there stunned for a few moments, not quite sure what to do about the scene that had just happened before them.

"Bob, what should we do about her? I've never seen anyone freak out like that before."

"Nothing we can do, Bernice. Don't worry about her, she's just full of hot air. You can rest assured she's going to spread some wicked gossip around to discredit Jim though. We may have to tighten our belts a little if it hurts our business."

"What about Jim? What should we tell him?"

"We tell him nothing until we have to. Maybe it will all blow over and nothing will ever come of it. Let's just get back to work like nothing happened and let things fall into place as they may."

Neither Bob or Bernice felt like talking as they went about their business. Big Jim was working away out back, not knowing anything of what had transpired inside the store. It was only a little more than an hour later when the pair would learn Mrs. Messner intended on carrying out her threat. John Higby was the first customer to show up. He found Bob in the plumbing aisle and launched an immediate verbal assault.

"Korreck, what's this I hear about you hiring a criminal to work here?"

"Only honest people work here John. You should know that."

"That's not what I hear from Mrs. Messner. She said you have a dirty, long-haired, hippy freak biker out back. Probably hiding from the law or getting ready to deal drugs as I understand it."

"If that were true, I'd be kicking him out of here myself."

"Just the same, I came to load up my mower and take it elsewhere. I'm not going to have any of my money supporting that man's bad habits."

"Be reasonable, John. You don't know what kind of habits he has. Heck, I don't know what kind of habits he has. Let's give the guy a chance. He's actually been working on your mower this morning. How about we see what he's done so far first?"

"If it's torn apart, I'll load up the pieces. I'll have none of this Bob. None of it."

"I'm sorry you feel that way John. Pull around back and I'll help you load it up."

Bob was seething with anger inside as he walked out back. One thing he had little patience with was other people sticking their nose in where it didn't belong. He didn't really know what Big Jim had done in the past, but he knew he had believed in him when he was young and was willing to give him a chance now regardless of what his past held. It really steamed him when he thought about

Mrs. Messner spreading gossip around like that too. John Higby had fallen for it and he wondered how many others were going to be caught up in this web of deceit. There was no time to think about it anymore because John Higby already had his pickup truck and trailer in place and ready to load up his mower. John was already looking around when Bob walked up to him.

"Okay Korreck, where's my mower? I bet that criminal already stole it and sold it for drugs."

"John, I'll have no more of that talk in my place of business. I've been respectful and neighborly with you and I expect the same in return."

"Korreck, that mower is my property and it's my right to get to the bottom of its' disappearance." John Higby's voice was getting louder and meaner with each word.

"Now John…."

Bob's sentence was interrupted by the look on John Higby's face. His look of anger turned to one of surprise, astonishment, and was now starting to look like fear. Bob quickly turned to see what Higby was looking at. He soon understood the expression on Higby's face. Big Jim had been hidden behind one of the larger mowers and was standing up. He was imposing enough, but he looked downright frightening now that his jacket had been removed and his muscle shirt showed off his bulging muscles. With his boots on, he was probably more than a foot taller than Higby too. Bob searched Jim's face for signs of emotion because there was no way he could be able to stop him from tearing Higby apart if he wanted to. Thankfully his face showed no signs of anger as he slowly walked over to Higby, wiping grease off his hands with a shop rag as he went. Bob could see Higby was starting to shake as Big Jim towered over him and looked down.

"This might be fun to watch after all," Bob thought to himself.

"Name's Dunning. Jim Dunning," said Big Jim as he stuck his hand out to shake John Higby's, "is there a problem?"

"Uh....but....uh....I'm.....uh." John Higby was so scared he couldn't get any words out. His hand completely disappeared within the grasp of Big Jim's hand.

Bob was really beginning to enjoy what he was seeing so he played it up. "Jim, Higby came to get his mower. Says he doesn't want to fund any of your evil ways."

Big Jim just shook his head. "I don't have any evil ways Mr. Korreck. Uh, I mean 'Bob'. At least I don't any more. His mower's ready to go anyway."

"So soon? That's great! Where is it?"

"Right there," Jim said as he pointed to the mower right out front, "just start it up and drive it on the trailer."

John Higby suddenly found his voice again. "That isn't my mower."

Big Jim looked at Bob. "It's the one you told me was his."

Bob just shrugged his shoulders.

John Higby continued. "Mine looked like that one when it was new, but it's pretty well worn now. I know what you're trying to pull, you're trying to work the old 'switcheroo' on someone and I won't be a party to it."

John Higby quit talking very suddenly when Big Jim put his hand on his shoulder. "I think I know what's going on here, Mr. Higby. Let me show you what I've done."

Bob could tell Higby didn't want to see what Jim had done but was too afraid to argue. He was starting to shake again too.

"If you look over here," Big Jim said as he pointed to a dirty spot near the shop, "you'll see all the dirt that I washed off of this machine. I needed it to be clean before I started trying to figure out what was wrong. I used this air hose to help dry it off too. As soon as I looked at the wiring under the steering wheel I saw the problem right away. The hot wire was off of the ignition switch, so there wasn't any voltage going to the starter. I found the nut and washer in the pile of dirt I washed off, so all I did was clean it up and put it back together."

Big Jim now turned towards Bob. "If it's okay with you Mr. Ko..., uh, Bob, I don't think we should charge Mr. Higby for this simple job."

Higby's mouth was hanging open. "I still don't think it's my mower. It looks too new."

"You'd be surprised what a little bit of care will do," answered Big Jim.

Bob took a closer look at the mower. "John, looks to me like your initials are on this keychain. Same keychain that was on that dirty piece of junk you brought in. Looks like this 'criminal' did a pretty good job of working on it to me. Jim, if you say 'no charge' then I'll agree with you. You're the expert on this one." Bob made sure he gave John Higby a look of defiance when he said that.

John Higby didn't know what to say and stood there silent. Instead of waiting for a reply, Bob climbed up on the mower, started it right up, and drove it up on Higby's trailer. He and Jim had it secured and ready to haul away in no time.

Jim walked over to Higby. "There you are sir, all ready to go. If you want me to give it a good tune-up sometime feel free to bring it back to me. And thank you for letting me work on your mower, sir."

John Higby practically snarled out his words. "Don't hold your breath waiting."

"What did you say?" Jim's back straightened up and there was a little bit of meanness in his eyes as he stood toe-to-toe with Higby and looked down on him. He wasn't going for fear, but that was the effect his question had. Higby started to shake again.

"Uh...nothing....I didn't say anything," he said, slowly stepping back from Jim at the same time. The fear was obvious in his voice.

Bob quickly stepped between the two men.

"Thank you for your business John. Have a nice day and feel free to stop in again."

This time Higby kept quiet and just got into his truck and drove away, making sure Bob and Jim were in his rear view mirror as he pulled out.

"That's your church folks for you."

"What do you mean?"

"Didn't you say before that you followed Jesus?"

"Yeah."

"Well, so does that guy." Bob turned, kicked up some dust and headed back to the store.

In the next few hours there were a handful of other people that showed up and took their things with them. Big Jim had an idea what was going on, but Bob didn't look like he was in any kind of mood to discuss the matter. Jim just tried to keep his mind occupied with each task in front of him and not think about what was going on. Still, between what was going on here at the shop and what had gone on with Joshua the night before, Big Jim was feeling an anxiety inside like he had never felt before. The tension just kept building up inside him as the day wore on and he was more than happy to see Bob coming back at the end of the day so he could get to the bottom of what was going on.

"Okay, Bob. Just what's been going on around here today?"

"Nothing. Nothing at all."

"Don't give me that. What's up? Why are people showing up and taking their stuff away?"

"It doesn't concern you."

"Really? I'm thinking that at least a little of it must have something to do with me."

Bob looked down at the floor. It was obvious to Jim that he was thinking hard about what to say next.

"Well, yes, I think it does have something to do with you. But it's nothing I can't handle myself."

"I like to take care of my own responsibilities, thank you very much, so just let me in on what's going on and I'll take care of it."

"If you really must know, a customer threatened to harm my business if I let you work here."

Big Jim was silent. In the past, this sort of treatment was what he was used to, a part of his everyday life. He thought all that was behind him since he found salvation and he turned his life around. People had been treating him differently since then and he thought that was how it was always going to be. This caught him totally off-guard and he wasn't sure what to do.

"Bob, if I'm the cause of this, I'll leave. I don't want your business to suffer because of me."

"Don't you be telling me how to run my business. It's my decision who works here and who doesn't. So what if a few people thumbed their noses at us? It's pretty obvious to me that you know what you're doing and have done a really good job on what you've worked on here. In time the customers that left will be replaced with others. I'll have no more of this nonsense from you!"

"I don't want any trouble because of me Bob."

"You're not the cause. You're just the object of the hatred. I have little tolerance for such narrow-minded people and I refuse to let them run my life. I expect you to be here again tomorrow, bright and early. Is that clear?"

"I'm not sure that's a good idea Bob. I really don't want any trouble. I don't mind folks targeting me, but I don't want them taking shots at you just because of me."

"I'm going to say this one time so listen carefully. You are not the problem. They are. Be here tomorrow, understood?"

"If that's what you want."

"That's what I want."

Big Jim wasn't quite sure what was taking place, but he could tell Bob was getting very angry so he decided not to push the issue. He was just happy the day was over. "I'd probably feel a lot better if I went over and talked with Max about this," he thought to himself, "this all feels really strange."

7
GOSSIP

Margaret Messner had been a busy lady. She left the hardware store and went straight to John Higby's house to plead her case against Big Jim, or as she called him, "that animal." It was a stroke of luck that Higby had equipment there to be repaired that he could go and get. Taking that business away from the hardware store right off the bat would surely prove her point to that stubborn Bob Korreck. He'd surely reconsider keeping Big Jim if there was no more work for him. She wouldn't rest until she was sure "that animal" was run out of town. To make sure that would happen, she set herself on a course to visit as many members of her husband's congregation as she could and spread the word. She was getting pretty good at reciting her entire case against Big Jim by the time she had reached the Spicher's house.

"You know we can't just give people like that a foothold in our community." The way Margaret hissed out the words would give one the impression she was talking about evil incarnate. "It will start slowly at first but get bad fast," she continued. "It could begin with simple vagrancy. Then maybe progress to shoplifting. Next thing you know, it's burglary, drug-dealing, and who knows, maybe even murder."

The Spichers were hanging on Margaret's every word and she could tell her speech was having an impact. As their eyes widened, she became more passionate with her speech.

"What of the children? What will happen to our children if we let beasts roam around like that? Such a bad influence cannot be tolerated in our community. We must take action!"

There was a short, awkward silence before Bill Spicher spoke up. "The Warrens are friends of ours and they go to that church where the Carson guy preaches. From what I understand, he's pretty tight with that biker. Maybe we should tell them what you're telling us. After all, what kind of pastor would hang around with criminals? It can't be much of a church if people like that are in it. I've even heard that Carson's wife and that biker were friends. Hard to tell what's going on there."

"That's right! They must be informed. Invite them to come to our church where they won't have to worry about sharing a pew with a fiend."

"We'll call them right away. They need to know."

Like most small towns, the gossip spread like a bad disease. It was not beyond belief that the gossip would spread out into a public place such as the Town Center Super Market. It was there that Margaret Messner's tales reared their head in an unfortunate and ugly way.

"Did you hear about Preacher Carson's wife?"

"I heard she's cavorting around behind his back with that heathen biker. That has to be like dancing with the devil himself."

"Yes, and I bet he's working on corrupting those kids of the preacher's too. That kind of person just isn't happy unless they can drag everyone down to their level."

Max Carson heard every word of the exchange from the next aisle over. He had been ignoring the idle gossip quite well until his name came up. From that point on, each word hit him like a pointy dagger in his heart. The pain of each word grew until it finally became more than he could stand and he made a path directly for the front door, leaving his cart where it sat in the aisle.

Big Jim was already at Max's house doing what he usually did when he visited, playing tea party with little Mary. Most men would be afraid to be seen drinking imaginary tea with a little girl and her dolls, but not Big Jim. He was drawn to Mary's childlike innocence and her simple honesty, and quite frankly, he always felt a special bond with her since she always accepted him just the way he was. With all the trouble that was going on at the hardware store coupled with the burden he felt over Joshua's rebellion, a private tea party was actually just the thing to make him feel better.

"Hey, why don't you two party animals come in here for some milk and cookies?" called Emma from the kitchen window.

"Cookies! Cookies! What kind did you make momma?"

"Your favorite, sweetie. Peanut butter chocolate chip!"

"Yay!" Mary jumped for joy and ran to the house, leaving Big Jim sitting there by himself.

"Are you coming too, or do you need an engraved invitation?" Emma chuckled as she held up the tray of cookies for Big Jim to see.

Big Jim smiled and got up to head in for some cookies. He liked being able to see Emma, yet he still felt very uncomfortable around her. He hadn't had any problems with his old feelings for her coming back, but their past history still made any kind of a visit difficult. If it weren't for his growing friendship with Max and the bond he had with Mary and Joshua, he would probably just stay away from Emma altogether.

"Sit down here with me, Mister Jim."

Big Jim could tell Mary wasn't going to take no for an answer so he pulled out a chair next to Mary and sat down.

"Have a cookie, Mister Jim, these ones are my very most favorites!"

"Well then, if they're your favorites, they'll have to be my favorites too." Big Jim smiled at Mary and shot a wink at Emma.

"You two certainly look like you're on top of the world there with those cookies."

"Must be the cookies, these are incredible! When did you learn to cook like this?"

"I just kind of picked it up over time. You learn these things raising a family, you know."

"Well, that's something I really don't know anything about. I starting to wish that I did. This little girl of yours is a pretty incredible kid."

"Yeah. Takes after her mother." Emma was laughing.

Big Jim lowered his head and fixed his stare on his cookie plate.

"You're right. You are incredible. Only an incredible woman could've made such a good life from the mess I left you with. I am so terribly sorry for all the hurt I must've caused you. So sorry."

"Jim, I'd be lying if I told you it didn't hurt. It did. A lot. I don't know what would've happened if Max hadn't been there to help. I thank God every day that he was there for me. I have to admit that I hated you for leaving like you did too. It took a long, long time to get over that. That's something else that Max helped me with. He helped me to understand how God forgives us and how we need to forgive others too. It took a lot of effort, but I was finally able to forgive you, Jim. It's only through God's grace that I can accept you being in my kitchen and playing tea party with my child. God has also shown me how He's working in you Jim. The Jim Dunning that left me high and dry all those years ago is not the Jim Dunning that is sitting here before me. The old Jim Dunning is gone. You're a new creature, a new Jim Dunning."

"And you're okay with the 'new' me?"

"I'm okay with you as Max's friend. That sort of makes you my friend too by default. Between that and the way Joshua and Mary adore you, I guess I'm stuck having you in my life in that capacity. I think we can put the past behind us and just be friends, can't we?"

"I guess so. It still feels a little strange, but I'm learning to deal with it. I'm beginning to think it may not be such a good thing for me to be around Joshua anymore. I don't want to do anything that would make him turn into me."

"Where did that come from?"

"The other night at my place, Joshua was acting rebellious. It wasn't like him at all. I don't want him to get even worse by hanging around me."

"You give yourself too much credit Jim. Joshua is a typical teenager. He has been a bit rebellious lately, but they all get rebellious somewhere along the line. Even if he didn't have your genes, he'd still be fighting those typical teenage battles of growing up."

"Yeah, but those battles might be easier without me."

"Or maybe you can make him even tougher when he faces those battles. Before you came back, I was always dreading what I should tell him about you and what I shouldn't. Now I don't have to tell him a thing, you can tell him yourself."

"Some stories shouldn't be told."

"That would be your call."

"Tell me a story Mister Jim!"

Little Mary had been forgotten about while Emma and Big Jim had been talking. They both turned to see her smiling, cookie crumb covered face looking back at them.

"Please, Mister Jim, tell me a story!"

At that moment, Max came bursting through the kitchen door.

"What's going on here?"

The anger in his voice took everyone by surprise. Mary looked up at her daddy with an innocent face.

"Cookies, daddy. That's what's going on. Try one."

"Jim, I think you better leave and now."

"I don't understand."

"You heard me. Go. Get out."

"But I…."

"Go."

"But it…I don't….."

"I said go and I mean go now."

Max was visibly trembling with anger as he pointed toward the door. Emma was speechless. She didn't know what was going on and had never seen Max angry like this her entire life. Big Jim was equally shocked and surprised but he was already feeling bad enough and didn't want to cause any trouble, so he didn't say another word, getting up quietly and closing the door behind him.

"Daddy, Mister Jim didn't finish his cookies."

Max didn't even hear Mary and turned towards Emma with a look of anger.

"What was he doing here? What are you two up to?"

Emma's quiet shock was starting to wear off and she was ready to answer Max's fiery words with a few of her own.

"Pastor Maxwell Carson, you settle yourself down right now and tell me what it is you are up to!"

The harsh tone of Emma's voice settled Max down a little, but he was still angry.

"I heard some women talking about you and Jim down at the grocery store. Saying about how you two were up to something behind my back."

Max was expecting those words to bring a reaction from Emma, but the reaction he got wasn't the one he expected. Instead of finding the look of someone caught in the act, he found himself looking into the eyes of a woman who had just ratcheted her anger up to a new level.

"You mean this whole thing is about something you heard some women gossiping about down at the store? All of the sudden you don't trust me? You've become such a friend to Jim in these last months and you suddenly don't trust him either? Not only that, you chose to have this ugly scene in front of our little girl?"

Emma's eyes were still seething with anger as she looked Max in the eye. His own anger was rapidly fading. Her words were sinking in and he was starting to understand how badly he had been acting and what a mess he had made. Little Mary came up beside her daddy and tugged at his pants leg to get his attention.

"Daddy, didn't you preach something in church about gossip and friends once? Mister Jim is my friend. He plays tea party with me."

Max looked down at Mary's innocent face and the harsh reality smacked him in the face just as hard as if Big Jim had punched him there. His voice was shaking as he spoke.

"Yes. In Proverbs 16. A wicked man spreads conflict, and a gossiper separates close friends. You remembered right Mary. Oh Lord, what have I done?"

Emma could see Max understanding the truth without a word being spoken. Her face softened and she placed her arm around Max.

"I think the evil one threw you a curve ball, partner."

"Yes he did. I owe you a huge apology, honey. I should have known better. I do trust you and I let that gossip blind me. Can you forgive me?"

Emma gave him a hug and a little peck on the cheek.

"You know I can. Just see it doesn't happen again, okay? And don't forget that I'm not the only one you need to apologize to. You have some more work to do."

"You are so very right."

Max got down on his knees so he could be down on Mary's level.

"Honey, your daddy made a big mistake by coming in here and yelling at mommy and Mister Jim. It was wrong of me to do it and it was even more wrong to do it in front of you. Can you forgive me, sweetie?"

Mary gave her daddy a big hug.

"I forgive you daddy and I love you. Ann forgives you too!"

Mary pressed her doll's face against her daddy's for a pretend kiss. Max had to wipe a few tears from his eyes from the love his girls were showing him. Love he didn't deserve, just like his Savior's love for him. It was touching moments like this one that really made Max appreciate his Father in Heaven.

"I need to make some phone calls. Try to get ahold of Jim so I can apologize to him too."

Just then the kitchen door opened up. Max's mind immediately thought it was Big Jim returning and he was ready to run to him and apologize. It wasn't Big Jim though, it was only Joshua returning and the disappointment showed in Max's face.

"Wow, I'm sorry to disappoint you by coming home dad."

"I'm sorry, son. I'm not disappointed, I was just expecting someone else."

"So basically, I did disappoint you by showing up. Too bad for you. Say, what's up with Jim? I just saw him flying by on his bike real fast and he didn't even slow down or wave."

"That's my fault, son. I have to fix a bad situation now."

8
IN SEARCH OF JIM

Max knew in his heart that he had to get ahold of Big Jim and fast. He figured the best bet might be to call his father, Pop Dunning.

"Hello? Mr. Dunning? It's Max, is Jim there?"

"No Max, I haven't seen him all day."

"If he shows up, can you tell him to contact me immediately? I've made a terrible mistake and I must make it up to him."

"Sure thing, Max. If he shows up, I'll point him in your direction. You might want to try Bob Korreck over at the hardware store too."

"Thanks Mr. Dunning. I think I'll do that."

"No problem, youngster. Hope you find him."

"Thanks. Me too."

Max had hoped it would be easier than this. One phone call. Set up a quick meeting. Get this ugly episode behind them. Maybe it would only take one more phone call. If Jim wasn't home, he surely had to be at the hardware store.

"Miner's Hardware."

"Mr. Korreck?"

"Yes, call me Bob."

"Okay…uh, Bob. This is Pastor Max Carson and I'm looking for Jim Dunning. Would he happen to be there?"

"No, I haven't seen him since quitting time. It's getting pretty close my quitting time too, so talk fast."

"Do you have any idea where he may be?"

"No. You sound a little desperate, is there something wrong?"

"We had a bit of a disagreement. I need to get it straightened out."

"Well, if I see him, I'll let him know you're looking for him."

"Thanks, Mr. Korreck. I really appreciate it."

"Call me Bob. It's no problem. Really."

Bob's mind was racing before he had even hung up the phone. He knew Jim was a little out of sorts when he left work and if there was another problem afterward….well he just didn't have a good feeling about any of it. He closed up the store right away and went out to try and find Jim.

Max had exhausted all of his hunches on where Big Jim might be. He called every place he could think of, even took a few laps around the neighborhood, but there were no signs of him to be found. It had been a long day and after numerous trips of pacing around his living room he decided to call it a night. Emma had already gone to bed several hours earlier and her rhythmic breathing told him that she was sound asleep. It felt so good to lay down. Every ounce of him welcomed the comfort of the soft, warm bed. Sure, he was still worried about Big Jim and what had gone on that evening, but he was so exhausted that sleep would come, and it came quickly. Max was sound asleep in a matter of minutes.

"Daddy?"

The voice seemed like a dream to Max. But it wasn't. But was it real? He was in such a deep sleep that reality wasn't something he could easily comprehend.

"Daddy? You need to wake up daddy."

The voice wasn't stopping. Where was it coming from? It seemed real but his mind was still telling him it was a dream.

"Daddy, wake up now!"

Max's dream world was about to have a collision with reality. Mary started poking his arm to wake him up.

"Huh? What?"

"Wake up daddy."

"Mary. What? What are you doing?"

"Wake up daddy, we need to pray for Mister Jim."

"Sweetie, it's late, you should be asleep in your bed."

"Daddy, we need to pray for Mister Jim."

"Honey, we pray for Mister Jim and everyone in our family every night, now go back to your bed and get to sleep."

"No daddy, we need to pray for Mister Jim now. He needs us."

The more Max became awake, the more he became aware of the urgency in Mary's voice. Her face wore a look of determination that Max knew from experience had to be dealt with.

"Okay, honey, let's kneel down and pray for Mister Jim."

The two of them kneeled down together beside the bed. Max peeked out of the corner of his eye to make sure Mary had her eyes closed before he started.

"Dear God, please watch over our friend Jim and keep him safe. Amen. We've prayed for Jim now, honey, so go back to bed."

"No daddy. We're not done yet."

Max wasn't expecting Mary's response. The resolve in her voice left him speechless for a few moments.

"Okay, sweetie, you go ahead if you have more to say to God."

He thought making her do the praying would stop her. He was wrong.

"Dear Jesus, please help Mister Jim. I know you love him. I know he's in trouble and bad things are after him. I know you can help him and take care of the bad things. Please send some of your angels to protect him and bring him back so we can play tea party again. You can come and play too if you want. Thank you Jesus. Amen. Now we're done daddy. Good night."

Mary gave Max a kiss on the cheek, picked up her doll and ran off to her bedroom, leaving Max there on his knees hardly believing what he had just experienced. He had just gone through the motions in his prayer and that precious little child laid it all on the line. There he was, still on his knees, feeling so very proud of his little girl and so ashamed of himself. He was a minister of the Word and his little girl had just had a more personal chat with Jesus than any he had in a long time.

After Bob Korreck had driven through the neighborhood once, he had a strange feeling he was looking for Big Jim in the wrong places so he aimed his truck down Route 17 towards New Bristol. Bob hoped his instincts were wrong. While Brooksville and Coalburg were sleepy little towns, New Bristol was exactly the opposite. Instead of streets full of homes, there were probably more sleazy motels and bars than anything else. The town merely served as a stopover point along the interstate for all kinds of different people passing through, many of them the wrong kind of people. Bob never understood it, but he always had seen the good in Big Jim when no one else could, even way back in high school. Bob still saw the good in him, but the way things had been going, he was afraid that Big Jim may have reverted to his old ways, looking to something familiar for comfort. Bob hoped he was wrong.

Bob slowed as he approached the first bar along the road. He knew he would have to drive slowly to recognize Big Jim's motorcycle among the others that were pulled up out front. The old building that was the bar definitely had character. The place was called Willie's Bar & Grille, but the only lights that worked in the sign above the door made it look like Wil Ba & Gr. Another sign said a band called Mama Jean's Boys was playing inside. Definitely a class establishment from the broken sidewalk right on up to the patchwork roof. Bob was starting to look over the row of motorcycles when he noticed a lone figure across the road. A rather large lone figure at that. Bob could tell for sure who it was when his headlights fell on the motorcycle. Big Jim was just sitting there on the bike in a relaxed position, looking at the bar. Bob got out of his truck to talk to him and try and figure out what was going on inside his head.

"Fancy meeting you here, Jim. What brings you to this neck of the woods?"

"Just tryin' to figure some things out."

"Things?"

"Yeah. Things."

"Pretty broad answer there, son. Do you mind getting a little more specific?"

"I'm not sure you'd understand."

"Maybe not, but try me. I've been around the block a few times and I like to think I picked up just a little wisdom along the way."

"If you say so. I was sure I had things figured out before I came back. Saw a whole lot of the ugly side of the world and didn't want to see any more of it. Thought life had no meaning. Then I came back to town and became a Christian. Everything changed and it was wonderful. Better than I could ever imagine. Lately things haven't been going well. My son, who I'm just getting to know, has gone from perfect kid to rebellious kid. You're losing business because of me. My friend thinks I'm up to something with his wife and kids. I was starting to think the last few months when things were good weren't real, that it was just a dream. Maybe it all was just a dream. Not real."

"And all of that is what brought you to the side of the road? Maybe it was all a dream. Maybe you just wanted to believe good things were happening. Sometimes that Christian stuff isn't what it's cracked up to be. Most of those folks that stormed out of the store with their business called themselves Christians. Is that the kind of person you want to be?"

Big Jim was a bit surprised by Bob's answer to his question. He took a bit of time thinking the reply over, studying the look on Bob's face before he answered him.

"Mr. Kor....I mean, Bob....I've always known you to be a fair man. It sounds like you have something against Christians. It's not like you to not give folks a fair shake."

Bob had some thoughts going through his head that hurt. Big Jim could tell there was pain in those thoughts just from the way Bob's face dropped, how he had to look away to avoid Big Jim's eyes before he answered.

"I was a church-going guy once. I was always there with my wife and kid every Sunday, every special event."

"I never knew you had a family."

"It was before your time, son. That so-called God allowed them to die in a fire. My so-called Christian brothers and sisters did nothing to help me through it either. Oh, some of them would say they were praying for me, but not one spent time with me when I needed someone to talk to. Not one was there when I had to try to put everything in my life back together. It was just me that had to get through it all. Yeah, I'm a little bitter about it to this day. Made me think it's all phony."

Big Jim could see tears starting to form in Bob's eyes from the pain his memories was causing him. It was clear to him now where that hard edge Bob had come from. He had also learned there was a soft heart beneath the tough surface and that heart was broken. Big Jim got off his bike and gave Bob a hug. That small act of compassion was all it took for Bob's tears to start to flow.

"I'm sorry. I shouldn't be letting you see me this way. The old hurt just doesn't go away."

"Bob, I want you to listen to me. It's okay. I still deal with old hurt too. Every day. Learning about that Jesus dude helped me to deal with it. With all I've been going through here lately, I was starting to doubt what I'd learned. It was really starting to hurt. I came here to do what I used to do, drown my sorrow with alcohol. I even went inside. It was hard for me to go through that front door, but I did it. When I was inside and looked around the room, I was nearly overcome by a wave of sorrow. Every face in the room looked empty. Either they were sad and trying to ease the pain or they were laughing trying to cover it up, but they all had an emptiness about them that I could actually feel. Some guy came over and tried to pick a fight to impress his buddies. He even landed a punch. I took ahold of him and I was about to knock him into tomorrow, just like I used to always do, but it didn't feel right. That's when it occurred to me that I was different now. I was changed. I saw how empty I used to be in that guy's eyes. I drug him back over to his table and sat him down. Told him to stop fighting people. Then I turned and just walked away with my back to the whole bunch. Probably a stupid thing to do, since they could've all ganged up on me, but for some reason they didn't. I didn't even hear any taunts or jeers or anything as I left. Just silence. I couldn't see anything, but I felt like someone or something had my back. Sitting out here thinking about the whole thing and then listening to your story makes me think that maybe sometimes we just don't see how God is working in our lives. Maybe it isn't Him that lets us down but it's his followers instead letting us down. Maybe lots of times we just let ourselves down. Max told me before about how this whole life is a battle between good and evil. Maybe we just don't accept that evil can fight against us.

Maybe we should stop thinking that God is only going to fill our lives with candy and ice cream. There's a war going on in this world and sometimes bad things will happen. I don't have answers for you, Bob, but I think I'm getting a better handle on what's going on. At least I'm trying to."

"I'm not sure I buy all that Jim, but I can tell you put some thought in it. As far as Max and people letting us down, you should know that Max called me trying to find you. Said something about a misunderstanding and needing to straighten things out. Sounded pretty desperate to get ahold of you too, like he felt really sorry about something."

"I'll look him up when I get back home. It's getting late Bob. Why don't you go home and get some sleep. I think I'm going to stay here awhile longer and pray for those people in there. I think they need someone watching over them too."

"Suit yourself, Jim. I want you to be careful out here and coming home. You don't know when some nutcase could wander out here and come after you."

"It'll be alright, Bob. I have a feeling I'm not alone. And thanks for coming here to find me. I appreciate it. I'll be praying for you too while I'm at it."

Bob just threw his hand up to wave as he walked away. He didn't quite understand it, but somehow he was feeling better inside after talking to Big Jim.

9
SPIRITUAL ATTACK

It was early in the morning when Big Jim's bike rumbled into the driveway at home. Through the darkness, he was able to see a light on in the kitchen and he knew instantly that someone was there waiting on him. Sure enough, as he walked past the window, he could see Pop Dunning seated at the kitchen table and it appeared that he was in prayer. Big Jim tip-toed up the steps as quietly as he could so he wouldn't disturb Pop. As carefully as he could, he opened up the back door and stepped inside. Pop still had his head down at the kitchen table and he could now see his brother, Brandon, slumped over in another chair in the corner obviously sound asleep.

"Good morning, son."

Big Jim was startled by Pop's greeting. He thought he had snuck in the kitchen so quietly he wouldn't be detected.

"You surely didn't think those big feet would be able to sneak in here without me hearing them did you?"

"Well….I guess not."

Pop laughed and got up from his chair and gave Big Jim a hug.

"It's good to see you son. People had been out looking for you. Bob Korreck stopped in here after he found you to let us know you were okay."

"There wasn't any need for anyone to worry. I was fine."

"We weren't worried. We've been praying for you through the night and had faith you'd be okay. Max called last night looking for you. I thought about how he was acting and called him back later to get the whole story. Seems there was quite a misunderstanding on his part and he really feels pretty bad about it."

"That's good to hear. What happened really hurt, and with what's been going on at the store on top of that, I was really in a bad way. I was just about to go down the wrong path when that Jesus dude got ahold of me again. Made me think a little more deeply about things and brought me back in line. I thought I had screwed something up with Max and then I realized that something must have happened for him to act the way he did towards me."

"That's right. Something did happen that brought it on. What's this thing at the store you're talking about?"

"Seems some folks aren't taking kindly to my working there. They've told Mr. Korreck that they'll never spend another penny in the store as long as I'm working there. I told him I'd leave and spare him any trouble, but he wouldn't have any of it. Got kind of stubborn about it."

Pop Dunning laughed. "Yeah, that sounds just like Bob alright. It also sounds like you may have rattled a few spiritual cages out there."

"What do you mean?"

"I mean, you give your life to the Lord, lots of good things happen in His name, and now things aren't going so well. You have trials. People are trying to get you down and kick you. Sounds like a spiritual attack to me."

"You really think so?"

"Could be. We live in a fallen world. Bad things happen every day because that's just the way it is since Adam and Eve left the garden. God doesn't save us from every little thing because He lets us make our own choices and live our own lives. He does want us to keep Him as the center of that life, though. When we do make our lives about him, that old devil doesn't like that one bit and tries hard to get us to lose that focus on the Lord. It just seems to me that's what's going on here. I've seen the Lord do a powerful work in your life, son, and you've been impacting others. It's quite possible the evil one is trying to derail that."

"I guess that makes sense. What do you think I should do then?"

"Keep your focus on God. Praise Him no matter if things are going good or things are going bad. If you keep your eyes on Him.....well, it says in the Word that all things work together for good for those that love Him. Sometimes we get to see the good, sometimes we don't. We just have to trust Him."

"That's what I've been trying to do Pop. I did lose my focus there for a little bit tonight, but I got it back. Maybe you should wake sleeping beauty there and let him know I'm home," said Big Jim as he nodded towards the still-sleeping Brandon in the corner. "I'll tell you all about what went on tonight after I get a little sleep. It's been a long night and I have to work in a few hours."

"I think I'll turn in too, son. We'll let Brandon figure it out when he wakes up."

Big Jim was asleep practically as soon as his head hit the pillow. He was already feeling at peace, but talking to Pop before going to bed really set his mind at ease and made for a deep, peaceful sleep. His sleep was undisturbed until his senses picked up that old familiar smell again. Bacon. This time he knew where he was and what was going on. Pop Dunning was making breakfast and by the sounds he was hearing, there must be company for breakfast too. The more awake he became, the more he was able to hear some familiar voices. It sounded like Max was out there along with Brandon and Joshua. This was surely going to be a good breakfast if the whole gang was here.

"Hey look everybody! The big ugly bear is finally done hibernating!" laughed Brandon as Big Jim came through the door.

"You should talk. You were doing your best sleeping beauty impersonation when I got home and it wasn't a very good one from where I was seeing it from," Big Jim shot back at Brandon without hesitating.

Max spoke up and cut them off. "You two clowns can have your insult duel later, let me get down to business and get some things settled first. Jim, I came here to apologize. I was wrong when I jumped all over you yesterday. I let a couple old gossips get under my skin and I should have known better. I was wrong and I am so very sorry. Can you forgive me?"

"That's okay, Max. I could tell something wasn't right because you weren't yourself. It wouldn't have bothered me much if I hadn't had such a strange day down at the hardware store."

"Yeah, Pop was telling me a little bit about that. Between what you and I have been going through, I'm starting to think that we may have a case of spiritual warfare going on here."

Joshua piped in, "I'm sure of it. I haven't been the best of people to be around lately and it was my fault for being self-centered and worried about myself. I lost my way for a little bit and I want to apologize to all of you for the way I've been acting."

Pop Dunning started to laugh, "youngster, you may have been poked around some by the fiery darts of the devil, but you have to realize there's a bit of stubbornness in your gene pool to deal with too."

"Hey," Brandon piped in, "what are you trying to say?"

"Yeah," Big Jim added, "what are you trying to tell us Pop?"

The whole group erupted into laughter all at the same time.

"Man, am I ever glad I'm not in the same blood line as you guys," laughed Max.

"It takes a special kind to handle our blood, buddy boy, and you ain't it!" laughed Brandon.

"Oh yeah, preach it my brother!" hooted Big Jim. All Joshua and Pop could do was sit back and laugh at them all.

"You're probably right, I doubt not many could handle being like you guys, but you know what? I think I can handle some of those eggs along with some bacon. How about we get this breakfast on the road? I'm starved!"

"Coming right up!" cackled Pop, "ready or not!"

"Nothing better than bacon and eggs to get the day started!" said Brandon.

"Correction," said Max, "nothing better than the Lord providing us with this meal, and us giving him all the credit for it."

"You know," added Big Jim, "you're right Max. If we're going to be fighting some spiritual battles like you say, maybe we should be gathering like this every morning. Get our day started off right."

"I think you're right on that, boy," said Pop, "let's make sure you and I make a habit of this and the rest of the gang here are welcome to join us whenever they want."

"I like that idea," said Brandon, "no one makes breakfast like you Pop. And I can't think of a better guy to go into battle with than that big, ugly hairball brother of mine."

"I have to be a part of this just so I can watch," laughed Joshua.

"Sounds like we have a consensus here," said Max, "count me in too. Let's have a prayer and get started here before our food gets cold."

As Max said the prayer, Joshua peeked at everyone around the table. It was a strange-looking bunch seated around the table, but he couldn't help but notice an inexplicable look of peace on all their faces. As he closed his eyes, a strange realization hit him. When he looked at Big Jim, there was a glow from the morning light surrounding his image. The only problem was the morning light was on the other side of the room.

10
WIN FREE SEX

The group had been meeting every day for two weeks for breakfast and Big Jim had gotten in the habit of praying for the rest of them before everyone else showed up. Big Jim opened his eyes after his prayer was done just in time to see Max coming in through the door.

"You seem troubled Max. What seems to be the problem?"

"I think it's part of our battle, Jim. I'm frustrated and I don't know what to do. There are so many kids in this town that I want to reach, but I can't seem to get through to them. Every time I think I'm reaching one of them, the call of the others seems to drag them back away. We've had decent numbers at our youth gatherings now and then, but lately things just seem to be falling apart here. Our youth meetings are practically empty and overall attendance on Sundays seems to be dropping steadily."

"Sounds to me like you're getting the same treatment as Bob down at the store. It's me they're against. Maybe I should just stay away for a while until all this blows over."

"Jim, we've talked about this before. You know I want my church to be packed every week, but I'd rather see only a couple people there for the right reasons than have it full for the wrong reasons. Your past has been wiped clean and there's nothing wrong with your present. This is just part of what we're fighting against and I refuse to let you give up."

Big Jim listened to what Max said and thought it over carefully before answering.

"When's your next youth gathering?"

"It's tonight."

"I have an idea. Do you mind if I do something to try and bring a couple extra kids in? I do have to warn you, that if my idea works, it may bring some…uh…non-church type kids in."

"There's nothing wrong with that Jim. All are welcome. If you think you have an idea that will work, I'll be behind it."

"Good. You just set up like you usually do and leave the rest to me. Mind if I drop in and give you a hand too? You may need it at some point."

"Sure Jim, no problem."

The conversation faded from Max's memory as the others showed up for breakfast and they had their usual spirited start to the day. Later in the morning, as Max was going about his usual visitations around town, it came back to him. Some of the people he visited were just as nice as usual. Then there were some of them that were polite but appeared to be very uncomfortable by his presence. The ones that really bothered him though, were the few like the Marshalls. They used to attend church regularly up until a few weeks ago. Max intended to ask if there was a specific reason they stopped attending and see if there was something they needed or something he could do for them, but he never got the chance. He knew they were home when he visited, but they didn't answer the door when he knocked. In fact, he noticed the light in the front room went off with his first knock and he could actually see the curtains part so they could see if he was still there. He was beginning to really believe all of this was centering around Big Jim after all. He didn't know what Jim had in mind for tonight's youth gathering, but his stomach was starting to tie itself in knots from a combination of anticipation and dread. That feeling was still there that evening when Max was preparing for the youth gathering. As he saw the first few kids coming through the door he wondered if they would be the only ones showing up, but then a few more came in behind them. Then a few more. And a few more. They kept coming until there were more than ever before. He didn't know what Jim had done, but he somehow managed to pack the place.

"Hey everybody, it's good to see all of you here this evening. For those of you who are here for the first time, I'm Pastor Max and I hope you enjoy yourself and learn a few things along the way tonight."

"We'll start having a good time as soon as the contest gets started," came a voice from the back of the room.

"Contest?"

"Yeah, it's on the big sign out front. That's why we're here."

Max really had no idea what they were talking about.

"Big sign out front?"

"Yeah, man, that's why we came in."

"If you all will just pardon me for a minute, I'll be right back."

Max knew the only way he was going to figure this out was to check out the mysterious sign for himself. He was more than a little apprehensive to see what was on this sign that had the power to bring all these kids in tonight, but he just had to know. He was not prepared for what he saw when he opened the door though. There it was at the end of the sidewalk, a big sign with three big words. WIN FREE SEX. Out there for all to see. Now he knew why all those kids showed up. He also had a pretty good idea why there was a group of people across the street huddled together talking, too. He didn't know all of them, but he could recognize Margaret Messner in the middle of it and it appeared that she was doing most of the talking just by seeing the wild arm motions she was making while talking. Max had a feeling he was in for a long night as he walked back in to face the kids. He was searching for the words to get this started as he walked slowly back in front of them. Words that wouldn't cause any kind of a scandal connected to the sign, either. Where did that sign come from anyway? He sighed and looked skyward hoping for some sort of sign as to how he should start.

"Gang, I'm not sure what to say here. I have a feeling that a lot of you are here for something you won't find."

"That's right, they are!"

Max was so startled by the unexpected voice that he didn't recognize immediately that it belonged to Big Jim, who had just made a surprise appearance from the side hallway.

"Most of you came rushing in here thinking you knew what you were doing, but you didn't really pay attention."

A rough-looking boy in the front row spoke up, "I paid attention. The sign said 'win free sex' and that's what I'm here for. Free sex."

More than a few of the other kids were murmuring among themselves in agreement and giggling. It was obvious a lot of them were here for the same thing. Max was starting to feel sick. He wasn't sure if he was happy Big Jim was doing the talking or not.

"I was a lot like you young punks once. Rush right into something without thinking it through. Not checking the situation out before diving in."

The kid in the front appeared a little agitated as he spoke again, "What do you mean we didn't check it out? The sign was pretty plain."

"You think it was plain, eh? What do you think it said?"

"You know as well as I do what it said. It said 'win free sex'."

"That's where you're wrong, young man."

The kids in the crowd looked a little puzzled now. They all thought they knew what the sign said. Max was just as puzzled as the kids.

"Well if that's not what it said, now just what did it say?"

"You didn't look closely enough. It didn't say win free sex. It said, 'WIN. FREE. SEX'."

"Same thing."

"No it isn't. First word. Win. Nothing to do with free. Nothing to do with sex. Everyone here wants to win, right?"

A few of the kids nodded their heads right away, a few of them nodded slowly, and others weren't ready to commit to where this was going yet. The regular church kids were looking really uncomfortable. Max had to sit down. It looked like the kid in the front was starting to enjoy this as he started to speak.

"No one wants to be a loser. How do we know you're not a loser?"

"I'm not a loser because Jesus fights my battles. Not even death could stop him. Even if I fall, He picks me back up again. Even if I die, I'll get to live with him forever. If that's not a win, I don't know what is."

The kid started to laugh, "you're not going to try that 'faith' nonsense on us are you? No one believes stuff they can't see. I trust in what I can do. Me. That's my faith. None of that invisible crap."

Big Jim walked over to stand in front of the kid in the front row.

"It's not nonsense. Faith is our evidence of things we can't see. There's a whole world out there that we can't see."

The kid wasn't backing down.

"Yeah, buddy. You know what you can do with your invisible world."

That was the wrong thing to say. Big Jim leaned down and put an arm on each side of the kid's seat and put his face down so he was practically nose-to-nose with him and stared him right in the eyes. The kid's rebellious attitude instantly faded and the color drained from his face.

"Look, kid. This is America. You're allowed to believe in nothing. But you will respect our beliefs here and you'll listen to me while you're here, understand?"

The kid just sat there with a blank look of terror on his face.

"I asked if you understood, young man."

The kid was still unable to get any words out of his mouth, so he just nodded.

Big Jim let out a bellowing laugh and stood up. "Good, glad to have you here, I hope you have a good time!"

Max just shook his head as Big Jim walked back to the front of the room.

"Okay gang, we've covered 'Win,' now let's talk about 'Free.' God's gift of eternal life is free. All we have to do is believe and accept that He sent His son, Jesus, to die for us and pay the price for our sins. We don't have to pay for any of the stuff we've done wrong because Jesus did it for us. All of it. For Free. There's no way you can think of a better deal than that."

Max was looking at the faces of the kids as Big Jim was talking. He was used to seeing blank stares and bored faces in his meetings, but they were actually paying attention tonight. He wasn't quite sure if they were buying into Big Jim's speech, or they were afraid of him, but they were listening nonetheless.

"Sex. What about the sex part? You surely can't talk about sex in the church can you?"

The kids really were listening to Big Jim and they couldn't wait to hear how he was going to handle the last part. Big Jim didn't even hesitate to answer them.

"You guys don't think the Bible and sex mix do you?"

"Ain't no way. The Bible is all about goody-good stuff, not the fun part of life," said a punk-looking girl in the front row.

"Any of you folks agree with her?"

It wasn't hard to see most of them were in agreement as they shook their heads.

"Well, you're all wrong. Wrong in more ways than one. Young lady, you mentioned the fun part of life. There's lots of stuff in that book about having fun in life. It even tells us that God wants us to live an abundant life. Not a boring life, an abundant one. I understand where you're coming from though, because I used to think the same thing you guys do. I've done lots of bad things in my life that I'm ashamed of and won't mention because they're not worth talking about, but I thought there wasn't anything wrong with it at the time. I did whatever I wanted and thought it was an abundant life, but in the end, it just left me empty. I always thought church people just sat around without smiling, not having fun, and just singing hymns. Boy, was I ever wrong. Since I started hanging around with Pastor Max over there, I've had more fun and an abundance of life far beyond anything I've ever had before."

"Yeah, yeah, yeah. Let's hear you tell us about the sex part. We all know church folk don't believe in sex or talking about it."

"Well, boys and girls, that just shows how much you don't know about the Bible. There's lots of sex in there. Rape, incest, adultery…..it's all in there. You'll also find it tells you all you need to know about the whens, whys, and why you shouldn't in there too. Sex will be part of God's plan for your abundant life if you do it His way. If you do it the way the world says is okay, it will mostly only bring hurt. I will admit there's a lot about it in the Bible I don't know. That's why you guys all need to show up here. Pastor Max over there is the one you need to talk to and learn from. He knows more about what's in the Bible than anyone I know and he'll help you to understand what's in there. Once you know more about what's in there, you'll learn how to get the most out of life. I was like you guys when I was your age. Thought I knew it all. So I did it all. And it left a big empty hole inside. I think some of you already know that empty feeling. It feels like something's missing but you don't know what it is. Pastor Max helped me learn how to fill my empty hole and he can help you with yours too. Give him a chance to show you what Jesus can do for you, just like he did for me."

Max scanned the faces in the crowd and saw that most of them were taking Big Jim's words to heart. One of the girls in the front row was quietly sobbing and he noticed a couple of the boys in the crowd quickly wiping a tear from their eyes when they thought no one was looking. He'd said much of the same thing many times when he ministered to youth, but he had never captured an audience the way Big Jim just had. Max knew this was his cue to jump in before they lost their focus.

"Jim's right folks, it's all about Jesus. Doesn't matter who you are, what you've done, or haven't done, it's all about what Jesus is in your life. I'm sure you've all heard things about Him and about church, but I can promise you that Jesus is so very much more than anything you could ever imagine. I'm still learning more about Him every day and I want to share what I've learned with you guys. We can learn more together and learn from each other as we grow stronger in Jesus every day. Don't be afraid to ask anything, and if you want to ask me something in private afterward, that will be fine too."

After that the meeting was far more dynamic than ever and Max was exhausted by the end of the evening. The kids were so engaged, that the meeting lasted an hour longer than usual. So many of the kids hung around afterward to speak to him privately that he thought the sun would come up before they were all done. Hearing Big Jim talking about church totally took the kids by surprise in a good way. Instead of ignoring the dull, old church people they had expected to hear from, they heard from someone they could identify with. As Big Jim's friend, the kids took to Max like they never had before and listened to his every word. It was exhausting, but it was also the most rewarding night ever.

"Had enough for one night Max?"

"Enough? Dude, you lit them up tonight! It was incredible how you connected with the kids."

"I thought the sign would be a good hook. You know, something that would reach the kids that wouldn't normally even consider setting foot in a church. After that, I just sort of made it up as I went. The Lord gave me the words, and I had you to do all the real work."

"I'm not totally sure I agree with your method, but I can't argue the results. The big test will be if they keep coming back. Can I talk you into coming back and helping the next time? The kids really seemed to connect with you."

"Well, I don't know if I'll be of any help, but I don't mind trying."

"Great. I have a feeling something big's on the horizon Jim."

"See you tomorrow, Max."

"Yeah, see you tomorrow Jim."

11
THE JESUS ROCK AND
AN OLD TRUCK

Pancakes were the order of the day at Pop Dunning's table in the morning. Max came through the door right about the same time that Big Jim showed up at the table.

"Well," said Pop, "I drove past the church last night and it looked like you guys had a lot going on."

"Pop, you had to be there to believe it," said Max, "it bordered on a miracle."

"Well, Max, you are in the miracle business you know," laughed Pop.

"You should've seen Jim in action. It was a sight to behold."

"Imagine that. Tell me about it Jimmy."

"I didn't do anything special. Max did all the hard work."

"You set it all up for me, big guy. You brought them in and got them ready for the Word."

Joshua spoke up, "tell Pop about the sign, he'll get a kick out of it."

"Sign?"

"Well, yeah, I made up a sign to get attention."

Joshua laughed, "it worked pretty good too!"

"Okay, I have to know now," said Pop, "what did this sign say?"

"Um…well….it said "Win Free Sex.""

"No!"

"Uh, yes."

Pop grasped the humor in the situation and cracked up. Brandon started to laugh so hard he couldn't speak and tears were starting to form in his eyes. Joshua couldn't help but laugh at Brandon and Pop. All Max and Big Jim could do was just sit there while everyone was having their laughing fit. They let the laugh-fest go on awhile till Max had enough.

"Okay guys. Enough is enough and I'm hungry. Let's get to these pancakes."

Pop took a few deep gasps to get enough air to reply, "say, did you guys catch the new centerpiece on the table?"

Max and Big Jim hadn't noticed until Pop mentioned it, but there, at the center of their table, was the old Jesus rock from Nanna Robinson's "secret place" for praying out back. Even though Nanna had been gone for a long time, her faith continued to inspire them and the Jesus rock was the symbol of her faith they rallied around most often.

"That's a pretty special touch, Pop," said Max.

"Yeah," added Jim, "that'll give our morning breakfast meetings some real focus."

"Not only focus, but a reminder," added Pop, "a reminder that what we pray for may not happen in our own timing but in God's. When I brought this rock in here, it made me realize that Nanna was faithful in praying for me and Jimmy both every day. She wanted us to be close to the Lord like she was and she prayed about it all the time. Now look at us here today. She didn't live to see it, but her prayers were answered. We have to focus on our goals in prayer and be faithful to let the timing up to God."

"Speaking of focus, how about we get going here? I'm getting hungry too," said Joshua, "breakfast prayer is on me."

It was tough for everyone to get through the prayer without snickering, but the smell of the fresh pancakes helped them to get through it.

"Well guys," said Big Jim, "I hate to eat and run, but I got to get over to the hardware store. Mr. Korreck has something he wants me down there for early today."

"Hate to see you go so soon, bro," said Brandon laughing, "but that means more pancakes for me. Just promise me one thing, okay?"

"And that one thing is?"

"No more signs."

That cracked everyone up and they were still laughing as Big Jim left for the hardware store.

Big Jim wondered why Bob Korreck wanted him to show up early that morning. Bob usually didn't hold anything back, but this time he wouldn't say what he had in mind. This was so unlike him. Big Jim wasn't really sure what to make of it. Things were really slow down at the store, and he was sure it was because he was there working for Bob. Bob was too headstrong to give in to the demands of those who wanted him gone, but he couldn't keep paying him forever if there was no business to bring money in. Maybe Bob was finally giving in and going to let him go. But then, he seemed so pleasant when they closed up shop the night before. Bob wouldn't make an effort to hide his disappointment if he were going to let him go. But what could be going on to make Bob so happy? Big Jim couldn't think of anything that had happened at the store that would have put Bob in any kind of a good mood. Big Jim's imagination was running wild as he parked his bike in the usual spot behind the store. He was glad the suspense of the moment would soon be over. It might be over sooner rather than later because Bob was sitting out back waiting for him.

"Hey, Dunning, it's about time you got here. I've been waiting."

"Okay Mr. Ko….uh…Bob, what's up? What do you want me here for?"

"We're going for a ride. Let's get going."

"Where are we going?"

"You'll see. Just get in the truck and enjoy the ride."

"Whatever you say boss man."

"Bob."

"Sure, Bob."

Bob left the store parking lot and headed out of town. The further they went, the narrower the road got. They were starting to see fewer houses too.

"Where you taking me, Bob?

"You'll see, Dunning, you'll see."

It was only a couple miles after that Bob turned down a dirt lane to an old farm house.

"We're here."

"Where's here?"

"My place."

"This is where you live?"

"What part of 'my place' don't you understand? This is where I grew up. It belonged to my granddad, then my dad, now it's mine."

"So what are we doing here?"

"I've got something to show you. It's out back in the shed."

The two of them walked around in back of the house to where the shed was and went inside. The old shed had the distinctive smell of mechanical history to it. A smell that spoke of old hydraulic oil, mold, and rust all rolled into one. The cracked window panes let in just enough light for Jim to see the form of an old truck.

She's not much to look at," Bob said quietly, "but she's still pretty solid. I think you might be able to get her running well enough to run around town in."

"What are you saying Mr. Korreck?"

"Bob."

Jim shook his head.

"Okay….Bob….what are you trying to tell me?"

"This old truck belonged to my dad. It was his very first truck. He bought it used when he was young and it served him well till he parked it here and got a new truck. When he got too old to drive on the road, he got it back out again and drove it around here on the farm. He said he felt alive again driving the old truck around through the fields. It was his ticket to freedom when he was young and again when he was old. It's been sitting here ever since he died."

"I'm afraid I still don't follow you..uh...Bob."

"I miss my dad a lot Jim. I still talk to him nearly every day. I don't know if he hears any of it or not, but it makes me feel good thinking he does. Sometimes I feel like his spirit is still hanging around here just looking to help us out. Anyway, last night when I was talking to him, I got a feeling that he would want you to have this truck."

Jim was stunned. He stood there silently trying to come up with something to say but no words came to his lips.

"You're going to catch flies if you keep that big mouth of yours hanging open like that son. Say something."

"I...don't know what to say. This is more than a truck, it's a family heirloom. I can't accept something that's such a big part of your life."

"Blast it! I have fond memories of dad in it, but to me it's just an old truck taking up space. I have no need for it and I already have a perfectly good truck. Dad and I both want you to have it and put it to use so it doesn't just sit here and rust away to dust."

"Sounds like you won't take no for an answer."

"That's right, I won't, so you may as well just accept it now and save yourself some time."

"Alright then, if you say so."

"I say so. Here's the keys."

"This is really special, Bob. I don't really know how to thank you."

"How about you just get her running and drive by and say 'thanks' when the time comes?"

"Deal."

"Now that we have that settled, let's get back to the store. With any luck, we'll have work to do."

"I don't know how you can keep your cool with all of those people staying away because of me."

"I've told you before. The day they can tell me who can and can't work for me will be the day I give it up. As long as I can keep the doors open, you have a job with me."

"If you say so, Bob."

"I say so."

The ride back to the store was mostly quiet. Big Jim mostly thought about what it would take to get the old truck working again. Bob was thinking about what Big Jim had said. How much longer could he keep the doors open with no business? He was always one to stick to his guns and keep his principles intact, but unless things picked back up, he would have to close up shop. That thought was still bouncing around in his head when they pulled into the empty parking lot.

"Well boss man, what do you want me to get into today?"

Big Jim looked over at Bob, but he wasn't answering.

"Bob? You okay?"

"Yeah, I'm okay dag nab it. This just kind of snuck up on me. We've always had so much work, I had to think about it. Prioritize things. Figure out what came next. Things have dwindled down so much that there's really nothing for you to work on. I guess you can take your pick. Want to mow the grass? Sweep up? Do a little painting?"

"Bob, really, if you don't have enough work, I can go home and you won't have to pay me."

"Hey, I'm the boss here, and if I want to pay you to sweep, I'll pay you to sweep."

"But if there's no work…."

"Now you stop right there. You and I both know why our work is going away. Those churchy do-gooders are spreading word around that no one should come around here because of you. Well, I believe in you no matter how you look and I won't let them push me around. You will work for me as long as you want to and I have a store."

"Easy, Bob, no reason to get in an uproar. How about I clean and organize the tools and equipment today? If there's any time left, I'll start cleaning up around the outside of the store."

"I'm sorry for the outburst Jim. It's just so unfair what they're doing to you and I have so little patience for such narrow-minded people. It drives me nuts."

"How about we just forget about those folks and enjoy the gift of today. Maybe this is the day things turn around and more people come in."

"I'm not holding my breath. We'll go about our business as usual, though."

It turned out to be a long and boring day at the store. One man stopped in for plumbing supplies, but there was no other business. Big Jim had the workshop spotless and the tools were cleaner than most folks' silverware. Bob spent most of his day just pacing around the store trying to keep out of Bernice's way. He was wandering around in the paint section when Big Jim found him.

"Quitting time, Bob. I'm going to go home and grab some tools and head back to work on that truck. Do you think it will run?"

"Your guess is as good as mine, Jim. It sort of ran when it was parked. I have no doubt that you'll have her back in top shape in no time."

"I hope you're right, Bob. I think it will make a sweet ride if I can get her going."

"You will, Jim. You will."

Bob watched as Big Jim rode off down the road on his bike. He really hoped Jim could get the old truck running without much trouble because he was really needing to have a reason to celebrate something.

12
MORE ATTACKS

Big Jim could see Brandon sitting in a reclining lawn chair outside the house as he was pulling into the driveway. He was happy to see him there waiting because they hadn't gotten to spend much time together since Big Jim had started working. From the look on his face, Brandon was happy to see him too.

"Hey, Big Ugly, what's up? Have a good day down at the ol' salt mine?"

"Every day is gift, my brother. This one was pretty much on the boring side, but it was a gift nonetheless. What's new and exciting in your world?"

"Well, these socks are new," said Brandon as he held up his feet to show Jim, "and I guess it depends on your point of view, but they can be pretty exciting too. I had the time of my life the other night just organizing my sock drawer."

Big Jim just shook his head and laughed, "one of these days I'll learn not to ask."

"So what do you say we do something this evening a little more fun than comparing socks? Got any ideas?"

"Funny you should mention that. The good Lord just used ol' Mr. Korreck to bless me today with a truck. Needs some work, but I think it will be salvageable. After I gather up some tools, do you want to come along and help me work on it?"

"Sounds like an excellent plan, brother. Should be a piece of cake with two experts like us on the job."

Pop Dunning popped his head out from behind the back porch and laughed, "with two experts like you two working on it, no one will be safe!"

"Hey Pop! How long have you been spying on us?"

"Long enough to know there's probably going to be another vehicle in the driveway soon. I have faith you guys will be able to fix anything. I suppose you boys will want me to put off supper to later so you can get started on it."

"You suppose right," said Big Jim, "as soon as I grab some tools, I'm going to head on over there and see what I've got to deal with."

"You mean what 'we' have to deal with buzzard breath. Don't leave me out of the fun."

"Oh, that's right. I'll have to deal with the truck and you both. Lucky me."

"That's right. You are lucky to be blessed by my presence. And don't you forget it."

"I'm sure you won't let me forget it. Or your magic socks."

"Magic socks?" asked Pop.

Brandon and Big Jim both cracked up laughing.

"You had to be there," Big Jim got out between laughs.

"Some people's kids," laughed Pop, "I'll leave you two to get on with whatever it is you and your socks are going to get into. Don't stay out too late if you want to eat tonight."

"No way I'd miss out on one of your meals," said Brandon, "and one look at this ugly guy's belly tells you he probably hasn't missed a meal in his life."

"We're just going to go over the basics tonight, Pop," said Big Jim, "mind if we take your truck over to carry the tools in?"

"Go right ahead, I'm not going anywhere tonight. Just keep it between the white lines."

"Will do. I'll drive her like an old lady."

Brandon laughed, "you always drive like an old lady, scum lips."

"Keep it up. I'll see that you walk home. Now be a good boy and go grab my tool box for me, would you?"

"Yeah, yeah, I'm on it. Let's go get to work on that new ride of yours."

Big Jim was already in the truck ready to go when Brandon loaded the tool box into the back of the truck. When Brandon got into the truck, he thought something was bothering Big Jim by the look on his face. He was sure something was bothering him by the time they had traveled a full mile on the highway in silence.

"Okay, bro, tell me what's up."

"What do you mean?"

"Listen, dude, I can tell something's bothering you. Let me in on it and get it off your chest. Maybe I can help."

"I doubt that."

"Try me. You might be surprised. If something's bothering you, don't keep it all bottled up, bro. I'm here for you and so is Pop, Max, and Joshua. Whatever it is, you're not alone in this."

"Okay, I guess this is the only way to shut you up. We're going to work on a truck that I've been given. I didn't to a thing to earn it. It's old, it's rusty, and it's about as wonderful an old truck as I could ever dream of owning and it's mine all from the kindness of Mr. Korreck's heart. What do I do to repay that kindness? I scare away all his business. Great way to thank him isn't it it?"

"I'll give you one point, you are pretty scary. But you're not to blame for what's going on down at the store. You know it's a spiritual battle going on."

"Yeah, I know. But I'm having trouble with that. It seems like everything I touch these days falls to pieces. Remember when I first came here? Everything worked.

Things just kept getting better every day. Now it's the exact opposite. I don't get it. Why isn't God watching over all this? He was taking care of us before wasn't he?"

"Dude, he took care of us then, and he's taking care of us now. The thing you have to remember is that it's the evil one that runs this world. As Christians, we'll never be part of this world, we're strangers in it. Remember back when I was sick and I kept going downhill? We didn't see any results but we kept on believing and it all worked out. Let me tell you, I had a lot of doubt on some days so I know exactly how you feel."

"I think I know where you're coming from, but this is different. If it was just me, I'd be fine, but I can't stand others getting hurt because of me. Mr. Korreck's been nothing but great to me and I'm causing him to lose business. It not only hurts him, but it will hurt Bernice, too, if she loses her job at the store."

"There's more at work here than just you. We'll just have to ride this out and see what God has in store for us in this situation."

"I guess you're right. But lately I almost feel like there's no one listening to my prayers. I have to keep reminding myself of the miracles we've seen in the past to remember that all this is real."

"Just keep remembering that bro. It all happens in God's time, not ours. This will all work together for good in the end. We just have to get there."

"Well, I don't know about getting 'there' but we've gotten 'here' so let's see if working on that old truck will help take my mind off of things."

"Well, one thing's for sure big ugly brother, even if it takes your mind off of things, it won't make you any better looking."

"Shut up and get the tools, would you?"

The old truck was still setting there just like Big Jim left it, yet it looked different now somehow. Now it was his truck and that made the flat, pale-colored paint look brighter and shinier to his eyes. He ran his hand gently across the front fender and felt a few nicks and small dents but it all felt good beneath his fingertips. A smile came upon his lips as he lifted up the hood to look at the engine.

"Wow! I'm glad I was here to see this, or I might not have believed it," laughed Brandon, "big ugly guy meets big ugly truck and falls in love. A match made in heaven!"

"Shut up and hand me my spark plug socket, buzzard breath. I want to get an idea of what we're dealing with here."

"We're dealing with an ugly old truck."

"It's better looking than you."

"You're a fine one to talk shovel face."

Brandon had worked on more than a few engines himself, but he always marveled at how Big Jim could work magic on mechanical things. It was incredible to watch how smoothly and quickly he had the spark plugs out of the engine. Big Jim examined each spark plug thoughtfully, without giving Brandon any kind of clue as to what he was seeing. After that examination, Brandon watched as Big Jim grabbed the fan belt and gave it a pull. Big Jim appeared to be looking over some of the wiring before he stopped and turned to face Brandon.

"I think this will do nicely."

"Nicely?" asked Brandon.

"Yep. This old girl seems to be solid. With a little fresh gas and a new battery, I don't think we'll have any trouble getting her running."

"Really? As much dust as is on this old thing, I figured it would almost be a lost cause."

"I'm surprised myself just how good this old truck is mechanically. I think we only need to spend another evening to get her up and running."

"Wow. You'll be cruising in no time."

"Yeah. I'll be able to give the old bike a break now and then. Hey, let's get out of here and call it a night. Let's drop by and see Max on the way home."

"Sounds like a plan, bro. You really think you can get this old thing running that soon?"

"I'm almost sure of it. These old engines are practically bullet-proof and I can see that this one was taken care of."

Brandon hopped up in the truck. "And you're just the big, ugly guy to keep taking care of it."

"I hope so," said Big Jim as he closed the truck door behind him, "I certainly hope so."

It was a short and quiet ride from the farm back to Max's place. They were both in a pretty good mood from the fun they had working on the old truck. Big Jim was anxious to tell Max about how good the truck was and how they were going to get it going. They didn't know it then, but their good mood was going to soon change when they found the unexpected scene they would be confronted with at Max's place.

"What's going on outside the church?" asked Brandon, "it looks like some sort of mob or something."

"I don't know," replied Big Jim, "but it doesn't look good. Let's check it out and see what's going on."

Brandon pulled up to the sidewalk in front of the church where the crowd was at. Big Jim wasted little time getting out of the truck and confronting the first person he came to.

"What's going on here? Where's Max?"

The old man that was on the receiving end of Big Jim's piercing stare was too frightened to move, let alone answer. He might have stayed there frozen forever if some of the others hadn't started to gather around.

"There he is! He's the one!" The voice of Margaret Messner rose above the murmuring of the others. "He's the one that brought evil into our town!"

Big Jim was stunned. He'd been called lots of names in lots of places, but it had never stung him to his core like this time. He could almost imagine this group of people around him picking up torches and pitchforks to drive him out of town just like an old-time movie monster.

Margaret continued. "We'll tell you what's going on, Mr. Dunning. You're like a curse, a plague on our town. Your kind always brings bad things and bad people. We're picketing this church until you're driven out. We know Pastor Carson is responsible for encouraging your stay here, so that just makes him part of the evil. We have witnesses here that saw your disgusting sign here at this church the other night. We can only imagine what horrible things went on inside this so-called church that night. We'll probably see all kind of shady characters coming into town now. Drug dealers, hardened criminals, probably murders and who knows what else. Most of the people here have already had things stolen from their properties. You're probably using that hardware store as a front for selling stolen merchandise. We know you're responsible for all the thefts because we've never had trouble like this around here before you came to town. Why don't you just leave so we can forget any of this ever happened?"

Margaret finally paused to catch her breath long enough for Big Jim to speak.

"Ma'am, I can't deny I've done some things in the past that were wrong, but I'm not that person anymore. I've changed. My sins are washed clean and I have a new heart. It's true that some people may have found my sign offensive, but it did reach a lot of kids who wouldn't have set foot in a church otherwise. It's not right that you're accusing my friends, Max Carson and Bob Korreck, of wrongdoing just because they know me either. They're both great guys and you can't be accusing them of things that aren't true, they deserve better than that. You're just hurting Max's church here and Bob's store. As far as thefts, I don't know a thing about that. Maybe you just need to take better care of your stuff, I don't know."

Max had been inside the church praying when he heard some of the noises that was coming from outside. When he looked out the window and saw what was going on, he rushed outside as quickly as he could. He made it just in time to hear the end of Big Jim's speech and get himself in between Big Jim and Margaret.

"All right, I'm afraid I'll have to ask all of you folks to leave."

"Pastor Carson, that's hardly a Christian attitude." The look on Margaret's sneering face as she spoke was downright chilling.

"Say what?" Max was caught off guard by her comment and was speechless.

"You heard me Pastor Carson. We're decent law abiding Christians expressing our freedom of speech. We care about our community and we just want to clean up some of the garbage that you've brought into your church and this community. You should be joining us instead of defending this...this beast the way you do."

"You want me to ....to what?" Max still couldn't believe what was going on. He had set out to keep Big Jim from getting angry and now he was the one starting to get mad. He could feel the color rising up in his face and he was about to lose his temper when Big Jim stepped in.

"Forget about it, Max. Let's just let this thing go and move on. Turn the other cheek. Let's go inside and put it behind us."

"That's right. You folks get off the street and let us God-fearing Christians clean up the town." The arrogance in Margaret's voice put Big Jim over the edge. He turned so fast that everyone was caught off guard. There was a sound coming from his throat that sounded a little like a growl and more than one of the mob turned and ran when he started to step towards Margaret. Margaret had lost all of her boldness when she saw Big Jim's snarling figure coming towards her, but she was too scared to move. Luckily Brandon and Max got ahold of Big Jim before anything happened.

"Come on, bro, let's just settle down and get out of here, okay?" Brandon's voice trembled a little when he spoke. He wasn't afraid of Big Jim, but he was pretty nervous imagining what could happen.

"Yeah, Jim," said Max, "let's just all settle down and go back to the house."

Big Jim settled down and was letting Max and Brandon lead him into the house when Margaret's courage came back.

"Yes, you need to all go back inside and repent of your sins before it's too late for you," sneered Margaret.

Big Jim turned around with such force that Brandon and Max went flying like rag dolls. His steps were rapid and forceful as he walked back to Margaret. She was frozen with fear, but it didn't matter because Big Jim grabbed her arms so she wouldn't go anywhere and looked down at her so they were face to face. His eyes were so wild, so mean, that she feared her heart would stop beating.

"When you go home tonight, you get on your knees and give thanks to Jesus. It's because He's here inside of me is why I won't….I can't….hurt you. You remember to thank Him for that. I know I will."

With that said, Big Jim let her go and turned and walked back to Max's house. Max and Brandon were still on the ground, looking at one another in disbelief of the scene they'd just witnessed.

13
DOUBTS

Big Jim sat at the table, mindlessly rolling the Jesus rock around in his hands, his eyes fixed on it. Brandon had driven him home from Max's the night before because the incident with Margaret had him too upset to drive. Brandon and Pop Dunning were worried about him because they'd never seen him this way before and neither of them knew what to say to help him. They just sat here helplessly watching him, hoping he would end his silence and let some of his frustrations out so they could help. Finally he spoke.

"I should've never come back. Messner's right, I brought all this trouble here."

Pop replied softly, "don't say that, son. Messner's wrong. There's been some really good times here that would've never happened without you."

"That's right," Brandon added, "if you hadn't come back, we wouldn't know about being brothers. I probably wouldn't be alive, either."

"Yeah, there were some good times, but the good times seem to be over. There for a while, I felt like I could feel God's hand on me all the time. Lately I don't feel anything. Did I dream the whole thing? Did God get tired of me and move on? I just don't' know."

"Bro, we've seen some real miracles here. It's all been for real. I'm sure God hasn't left us."

"I wish I knew that for sure," said Big Jim, his eyes fixed on the Jesus rock, "I just wish I knew."

"You know, I think you need to just be still son," said Pop, "seek that still small voice of His inside you. The more you fret, the harder He is to hear."

Big Jim looked up and saw the concerned looks he was getting from Pop and Brandon. After all the trouble that had been going on, the last thing he wanted to do was to be a worrisome burden to them.

"Maybe you're right, Pop. Maybe I just need to get out of here and be still for a while."

"I think it will help son. I think it will help."

"I guess we'll see won't we?"

Big Jim got up, still holding the Jesus rock, and went out the door. It was only seconds until they heard his bike starting up and pulling out of the driveway.

"Do you think he's going to be okay?" asked Brandon.

"I don't know son," replied Pop, "he's in God's hands now. The only thing we can do, and it is by far the best thing in this situation, is to pray for him. I think we all need to be doing it. Jimmy needs prayer right now."

Big Jim had been sitting up on Balanced Rock for over two hours, trying to hear the small voice Pop talked about. All he heard was the sound of Coal Creek flowing below, that and all the sounds of the scenes replaying in his head. All he could think of was the things that went on down at the store and at the church the night before. More and more he thought about the people who were being hurt by all of it. It was painful to think of how kind Bob Korreck had been to him, and now his kindness was repaid by a store that barely had any customers any more. Certainly not enough paying customers to keep the doors open much longer. Max was in the same position with his church. What was once a full, vibrant church now only had a few people showing up for services. All of this was his fault. Good people being hurt because of him. The pain, the anger welled up inside of him until he stood up and screamed, throwing the Jesus rock as hard as he could.

"Feel better now?"

The rock made an audible splash as it hit the water. Big Jim turned to find Joshua behind him. Now along with the pain and anger, he was also embarrassed.

"What are you doing up here?"

"Same thing I was doing the first time we met. Remember that day? I have some things I think I'm supposed to say to you."

"Oh, you do, do you?"

"Yes I do. Pop told me how upset you were when you left."

"I can take care of myself," said Big Jim angrily, "there's no need for Pop or Brandon to worry about me."

"Apparently, there is," replied Joshua calmly, "do you think this is the normal way you should be acting?"

Big Jim looked in different directions so he didn't have to look Joshua in the eye. "No."

"I think you need to listen to me, then. Just think about what I'm saying, okay?"

"I'm listening."

"Do you think the miracle we saw with Brandon would've happened if you weren't here?"

"We don't know that he wouldn't have gotten better without me."

"No we have no proof. But if you asked anyone, Brandon included, you would've gotten the same response. We all were pretty sure he was dying. We thought it was a done deal."

"So?"

"So it was your presence that brought on the miracle."

"I'm not God. I didn't do anything."

"No, you're not God. You didn't do anything, but you let God do all the work through you. Your presence made the difference."

"Okay. I made a difference. I served a purpose and now that purpose is over. God's moved on, so maybe I should too."

"You really think God's moved on?"

"I don't know what to believe. I do know I haven't seen him show up around here lately. Everything seems like it's falling apart."

"That's what the enemy would have you think."

"So you're saying it's not all falling apart? That things are okay?"

"We weren't promised a trouble-free life. There will always be trials. God will always be there to help you through the trials."

"Even when I can't tell He's there?"

"Even when you can't tell He's there."

"So what are you saying, then?"

"I'm saying you're down, but you shouldn't give up. The enemy thinks you're done, but God will give you what you need to get victory no matter how hard things look. Who do you think is planting all those thoughts of defeat in your head? Defeat doesn't come from God, you know."

"So what does all that mean?"

"It means quit sitting here with defeat and go back to being the guy that was leading us into spiritual battle, not running from it."

Big Jim let out a laugh. "Kid, you never cease to amaze me."

"Well, we're even then. I've never known anyone like you. I admired how you wouldn't let anyone or anything stop you."

"Well, I guess we have to keep that going then, don't we?"

"Yes we do. I have to admit it really scared me with you walking around acting defeated. I mean, if you gave up, how could I keep going on?"

"You're right. This hasn't been me at all. I can't believe I was giving up so easily."

"That's because you were letting it get to you little by little. The enemy is sneaky that way, slowly piling things on instead of slapping us in the face with one shot."

"Yeah, I see what you mean. I didn't even recognize what was going on. It was almost too late, too. Good thing you came along when you did."

"You think it was a coincidence? The pull of the Spirit to come here was so strong, I barely had to walk on my own. I felt like I was floating the whole way here. I had a good idea I'd find you here, but I wasn't sure."

"I guess no matter what we think, God's got it under control, eh?"

"That's what I believe. I see no reason to stop believing."

"I still have some doubts, though. How can I tell if it's me or if it's God working? How do you tell? You seem to be in touch with the Spirit."

"The truth is I don't know, Jim. I like to think I know sometimes, but most times, I'm just going by instinct. The closer I stay to God, the better those instincts are. Dad always tells me I have good instincts, but I think he's a little biased."

Big Jim laughed at that comment. "Kid, I think your instincts are right this time. I need to quit feeling like it's all falling apart and get back into the game."

"All I can tell you is that with all the bad things that are happening, there must be something big the enemy's trying to keep you from accomplishing."

"I don't know about that, but it would be easier if I knew what was going on."

"God will let you in on what you can handle. The thing is, we can't really handle the future or understand how his plan works. If we try to play it our way, we'll fail more often than not."

"I hear that. I've been doing a lot of failing lately."

"Maybe. Maybe your failures are all part of the overall plan."

"Well, I guess I better get back to whatever it is I'm supposed to do. Whatever that is."

"No one else can do it for you, you know," said Joshua with a laugh. "There's no one else out there like you."

Big Jim was still thinking of everything Joshua said hours later as he sat on his bike outside the bar. He still wasn't sure if he was doing what God wanted, but he did feel drawn to come back to the bar and pray for the people inside. He could see them coming and going. Some of them seemed okay, but far too many of them looked miserable going in and coming out. They needed to fill a void in their spirits and Big Jim was starting to really understand just what was needed to fill that void. Too many of the faces held the same look that he once had and he remembered what it was like to feel that emptiness. Sure, the alcohol took the feeling away for a while, but it always came back, sometimes stronger than it had been before. He could see now the difference Jesus had made in his life, even during the difficulties he'd been going through. It was more than a little embarrassing to realize how quickly he let that difference slip away when things got tough. While praying for the others, he also included a vow to the Lord to never forget that grace and forgiveness again. He had just finished up one of those prayers when the headlights of Bob Korreck's truck came upon him. Big Jim wasn't expecting a visit from anyone so it was a bit of a surprise when Bob pulled up beside him and got out.

"I thought I might find you here," said Bob as he walked over to Big Jim.

Big Jim laughed, "I'm not too hard to find if you look where I'm at. This is the second time today this has happened."

"What?"

"Never mind, you had to be there. What's up?"

"I wanted to tell you in person. I'm going to have to cut back on keeping the store open. There just isn't enough business."

"I'm sorry, Mr. Korreck. I know it's because I'm there."

"Bob. And get that notion out of your head. It's those blasted church people you like so much that's to blame. Not you. I don't understand why you want to be like them."

"Bob, I know people like that have hurt you in the past, and they're hurting you now, but please try to understand that all Christians aren't like that. I'm still new at this and I make mistakes, but it isn't Jesus that's making those people act like that."

"Ah, you're wrong. All those church people do is judge and criticize folks that aren't like them or don't do things the way they do them. That's why they don't take kindly to you, you're not like them."

"You do have a point there, Mr. Ko...uh, Bob. They don't like how I look, I know that. But Jesus doesn't judge me by how I look or dress. He doesn't keep me bottled up by giving me a bunch of laws that make me jump through hoops. He's forgiven me by His grace and I'm free to do the things He wants me to do."

"Sounds about the same to me."

"It's not quite the same. I had trouble understanding it at first, but then Max helped me to understand it. I'll try to explain it as best I can, but forgive me if it doesn't come out right. Those other people are living by their laws because they think that is what will get them to Heaven. I follow some of the same laws, but not because I have to, it's because I love Jesus and want to live the way He would want me to. I try to live through the freedom of the grace He's given me, not the bondage of laws like those other people do."

"That is a little tough to understand, I'll give you that. I've never heard it said like that either."

"Think about it, would you? You can receive that same grace too. I'm not good at explaining things, but Max has a way of making it easy to understand and I know he'll help. You need to release that old burden of pain you live under Mr. Korreck."

"Dag nab it, boy, how many times do I have to tell you to call me Bob anyway? I didn't come here for a sermon and yet you've got me thinking. Maybe there's something to what you're saying after all. I'll give it some thought. There'll be lots of time to think tomorrow since the store won't be open."

"Maybe you should go down to the store and pray over it."

"What in blazes makes you say that?"

Big Jim shook his head. "I don't know. It seemed like the thing to say. The words just popped into my head."

"Well, I'll just think over what you've said and see if anything pops into my head."

"Think about it real hard, it could change your life."

"We'll see. I better be going now and leave you to what you're doing here. Be careful, would you? This isn't exactly the safest place around to be."

"I'll be fine, Bob. You be careful too."

Big Jim watched as Bob Korreck got back into his truck and pulled away. He couldn't see the tears that were flowing down Bob's cheeks as he drove away. He also couldn't see the shadowy figure, hidden by the darkness, which had been watching them silently from a distance.

14
DWAIN HIGGINS

Big Jim had just started praying again after Bob Korreck left when he heard the sound of a motorcycle starting in the distance. Lots of bikes had come and gone during his time there across from the bar, but there was something about this one. The tone of the pipes as the engine roared to life had a familiar sound to it, one that his mind was telling him that he knew, but he couldn't quite place it. The mystery apparently wasn't going to last long because the headlight of the bike was coming in his direction. The bike was, indeed, familiar to him as the sight of an air-brushed bloody skull on the gas tank gave it away as it pulled in beside him. A cold feeling running up his spine told him the rider was familiar to him as well.

"Well, well, Mr. Dunning, it's been a long, long time. What have you been up to?"

"Hello, Dwain."

"That's the best greeting you could give your old buddy? Certainly you can show me more love than that, my brother."

"What are you doing here Dwain?"

"Looking for you, that's what. Some of the gang said you were acting strange when you left and I figured I should check up on you. See how you were. You weren't the easiest guy to find either, so you should appreciate the effort I've put in."

"Really, Dwain, why are you here?"

"You don't believe I care about you old buddy?"

"Not to the extent you'd come looking for me. Not unless you had some other reason."

"After all the fun times we had together? Remember that time down in the Carolinas when we trashed that bar and then the jail after they thought they could bring us in? You really beat up on a lot of people that night. Made me proud to be on your side."

"I'm not that guy any more Dwain. If that's who you're looking for, you best move along."

"C'mon, man. It'll be fun. Me and you, just like old times."

"Really? Tell me now, Dwain. Tell me what you really want from me."

"Well if you're going to be stubborn about it, I'll just go ahead. I want you to make a run with me. I could use your kind of muscle."

"A run?"

"Yeah, a run down to Florida. I've got a deal set up to pick up some stuff for delivery, and I might need a little protection. There's $25,000 in it for you for just for this run. You in?"

"No."

"No? Let me tell you, I've been spying on you for a few weeks. I've seen that you've lowered yourself to working at a hardware store, living in an old, run down house that should be torn down. Let's just live it up and trash that little town you're in and get back to the high life!"

"No. That little town is my town now and I won't trash it."

"It's ripe for trashing. I've been living off the fat of it the last couple weeks with no effort at all. We could do it up real good, just like old times."

"So you're the one that's responsible for the burglaries that have been going on lately."

"Burglaries? No, man, I've just been using stuff people leave laying around. Just borrowing from the rich to support the poor. Namely me." Dwain started laughing at his own joke.

"It's not funny, Dwain. Those are decent, hard-working people you're stealing from."

"What's wrong with you man? I watched a couple of times where it seemed to me like those 'decent, hard-working' people wanted you run out of town. They're not like us, Jimbo. We're different, we're free spirits, at one with the road and all that jive. You'll never be welcome in a place like this. Come with me on this run, you'll see, you'll be back where you belong."

"No. That's not my life any more. I don't belong in it any more. I'm never going to live that life again. I'm not the same."

"Man, you're sounding like you're on one of those goody-good hallelujah trips, like you've suddenly 'got religion' or something."

"No man. No religion. I'm following Jesus now, so I can't be a part of any of that old stuff we used to do."

"What? You're one of those wimpy people following that fake ghost guy?"

That was the wrong thing to say to Big Jim. He grabbed Dwain by his collar, lifted him up off the ground by that same collar, and slammed him up against a tree hard enough to knock all the air out of him so he couldn't speak. Big Jim was literally snarling as he looked directly into Dwain's eyes.

"Don't you ever, ever let me hear you talk that way about my Jesus again. Got it?"

All Dwain could do was nod weakly.

"And I want you to leave now and never come back here. Understood?"

Again, all Dwain could do was nod weakly. Big Jim relaxed a little and set Dwain down gently.

"Okay. I think we understand each other now. Good seeing you again, Dwain. Good-bye."

Dwain slowly regained his composure and looked at Big Jim in silence. If it were anyone else, he'd be furious, but this was Big Jim Dunning he was dealing with. The guy who had his back in so many fights through the years. The guy he'd watched mop up an entire room of attackers by himself on more than one occasion. The same old meaner than a grizzly bear look was still in his eyes, but somehow Dwain could tell there was something different there too. He wasn't the same Jim Dunning that he used to ride with. There might still be another chance later to try and connect with the old Jim Dunning, but Dwain knew the Jim Dunning that was standing in front of him right now wouldn't have any of that, so he quietly got on his motorcycle and left. Somehow both of them knew this wouldn't be the last time they saw each other.

15
BAD NEWS

Big Jim lost his mood to pray after the confrontation with Dwain. He didn't feel lost, but there was a strange feeling deep down in his spirit that he didn't recognize. It was kind of like despair, emptiness, and fear all wrapped up in one. Except he didn't feel down, empty or afraid. He kept going over the things Dwain said in his mind over and over trying to make sense of it all. When they were riding together all those times seemed good, but since he reconnected with his family and became saved, he looked back on those times as bad times, times he hadn't even thought about for a while. All those thoughts circled and circled in his mind as he drove home. He was distracted by these thoughts to the point that the trip was over without even feeling like any time had passed. He was happy to find that Pop was already asleep when he got home because he didn't feel ready to discuss what had happened with anyone. Maybe if he could get some sleep, things would be clearer in the morning. Sleep wouldn't come though. All the thoughts in his head would only allow him to toss and turn at best. Maybe he would be able to pray his way through it. It was hours before he would fall asleep in mid prayer.

Big Jim awoke the next morning to the sound of early morning laughter and conversation. It sounded like Brandon, Max, and Joshua were out there in the kitchen along with Pop having some sort of lively discussion. It always made him happy to have everyone around the table for breakfast, but on this morning, he wasn't sure if he wanted anyone around or not. The past he had put behind him was back and was crashing into his present and he didn't like it one bit. He briefly considered just lying in bed until everyone left, but there was a good chance they'd come check on him anyway. He figured he may as well go out and get it over with. Still, he paused before heading to the kitchen to join the rest of them. They never asked him about anything he did during his years away from home, a fact he was very thankful for. Now they might have to deal with what he was. Maybe the fear of them not accepting him after learning more about the things he had done was holding him back more than anything. After all, so many other things had gone wrong lately. Then the solution came to him. He remembered the pep talk Joshua had given him the day before and knew he had to straighten up his act. He had let down his guard and defeat had snuck back into his spirit without his noticing. It was time to quit feeling defeated again and move forward. The first step forward was to go out and face everyone.

"Wow, the ugly one's beauty sleep backfired," chuckled Brandon, "he got even uglier!"

"Yeah, good morning to you too," answered Big Jim.

Pop noticed right away something wasn't quite right. "You seem troubled Jimmy, those feelings of defeat aren't coming back around again are they?"

"They were, but now there's something even worse."

"Even worse? Tell us what it is then so we can help you."

"Dwain Higgins is in town. I saw him last night."

"Who is this Higgins character. I don't think I've ever heard of him."

"Be thankful you haven't. He's bad news. Real bad news."

"Sounds like you have some first-hand experience with this brand of bad news."

"Yes, I do, and it's very embarrassing to talk about it."

"It will help if you talk about it. We're all on your side here."

"Years ago, when I left this place, Dwain was the first guy I ran into. He sort of took me under his wing and protected me in the beginning. We rode together for years, getting into all sorts of trouble. Trouble I'm not proud of. Trouble I'd just as soon forget about."

"Nothing that can't be washed by the blood," said Max.

"I know that."

"But have you really accepted it?" asked Joshua. "You can believe it, but you really have to accept it too. He can't forgive you if you can't forgive yourself."

Big Jim wore a puzzled look on his face. "What do you mean?"

"Well, you believe that Jesus can forgive all your sins don't you?"

"Yeah."

"Once they're gone, He doesn't remember them at all. The problem comes when you remember it. That makes it just like His forgiveness never happened."

"I think I know where you're coming from. This is all because the enemy keeps reminding me of my past isn't it? Trying to keep me there so I can't move on into the future?"

"Yep. Just remember, whenever he tries to remind you of your past, just remind him of his future."

Big Jim laughed. "I had a pretty good handle on that until things got tough. So not like me."

"Well," said Brandon, "you're a new creature now. Just like the rest of us here. We have to put the old creature that was us back behind us every day."

"I have to do better," said Big Jim, "no more letting you guys down."

"You didn't let us down at all, Big Ugly. You let yourself down," Brandon said. "Now how can we help you with this Dwain person?"

"I don't know if any help will be needed. I sort of lost my temper a little and slammed him against a tree pretty hard. Something else I need to work on."

"What? Slamming people against trees? I imagine you're good enough at that," laughed Brandon.

"You know what I mean, goat breath. It's been harder to keep my temper under control lately. I even took ahold of an old lady the other night. I didn't hurt her, but I may as well have since I was thinking it."

"Don't worry about it son," said Pop, "we're all works in progress. From what I hear, I probably would've acted worse than you in that situation. We all have things to work on. Just keep moving forward."

Max spoke up. "What do you think brought Dwain to these parts anyway?"

"Me. It's me he was after."

"Why you?"

"He wanted me to run with him like in the old days. He wants to make a pick-up and wanted me to help."

"A pick-up? What do you mean by that?"

Big Jim hung his head. This was something he really didn't want to talk about. The others could tell so they didn't press him any further. They knew he would speak when he was good and ready to and not a second sooner. It was an awkward silence, but he finally spoke.

"Drugs. I used to help him make runs to pick up drugs to sell. That was one of the ways he would make money while we were on the road. I was okay with it at the time, but I know now how wrong it was. It makes me sick to my stomach to think about it now."

"Well, all that's behind you now, Jimmy," said Pop softly.

Big Jim looked up with a big smile on his face. "Yes it is. And do you know why? Because Jesus is all powerful and He's blessed me with such a wonderful family to support me!"

"Amen to that!" they all shouted together.

Big Jim slapped his hand down on the table loudly and laughed. "Now if you folks have had enough of this, can you tell me what it takes for a guy to get some food around this place?"

16
TROUBLE GROWS

The rest of the morning was pretty uneventful. After Big Jim finished breakfast, Pop went fishing while Big Jim, Brandon, Max, and Joshua worked on Big Jim's truck. The old truck seemed to be a perfect fit for Big Jim's personality, a rugged look and very sturdy. Joshua and Max both enjoyed helping out because neither of them had any experience with mechanical things and it was fun to learn from Big Jim and Brandon.

"Hand me that fuel line wrench, would you, oh great ugly one?" called out Brandon from beneath the old truck.

"How about I just drop it on your head? The only thing we'd have to worry about is hurting the wrench," replied Big Jim.

"Very funny, very funny. Isn't it enough for me to be tortured by the odor of your smelly boots while I'm down there?"

"Be nice or I'll take off the boots and you'll have to deal with the smell of my feet instead."

"Oh, the humanity! Okay, I give up, don't bring out the heavy artillery. For the sake of the free world, keep those boots on!"

Max and Joshua couldn't help but laugh at the free comedy show they were watching. This was definitely better than watching TV.

"You guys crack me up," laughed Joshua, "you two should take your show on the road."

"Maybe you should take your show on the road, young man," laughed Brandon from under the truck. "I suggest the road out front, right on the center line."

Big Jim's voice came from under the hood of the truck. "I love you guys. Thanks for being there for me when I need you to be. I've had trouble making sense of things lately, and I know I'd be a mess without you."

"Whoa! Serious moment, dude!" laughed Brandon.

"Jim, you've been there for us too when we've needed you. I know you'll be there if we need you again. We're all one in God's family," said Max.

Joshua chimed in, "that's right. Even though some members of the 'family' would rather kick you when you're down or judge you unfairly."

"That's enough, Joshua," scolded Max, "I've told you about having that kind of attitude."

"I'm sorry. It's just not right how they've been treating Jim around here lately."

"I know it's not right, but Jesus died for their sins just as much as he died for ours," replied Max.

Big Jim raised his head out from under the hood of the truck and stood up. "That's right, Max. I can't see it yet, but all this is going to work out in the end. I'm starting to see that a little more clearly now. Not everything or everyone in this world is lined up with God's plan. We just have to keep trying to follow God and let Him do the heavy lifting when we stumble."

"You would be a heavy load to lift. A big, ugly load at that," laughed Brandon.

Big Jim threw a wrench at Brandon, making sure it would miss him.

Max laughed at the two of them. "Never a dull moment with you two in the house. Now if you'll excuse me, I have to be getting over to the church to prepare for the service tonight."

Brandon rolled out from under the truck. "Do you think many will show tonight?"

"Well, the Morris family will be there. We'll be there. I'm not really sure if anyone else will be there or not. Our numbers have really dwindled down quite a bit lately."

"Yeah, I know. Doesn't it make you discouraged? I mean, my big, ugly brother here has been pretty discouraged, and we've all pitched in to support him, but what about you?"

"Brandon, I'd be lying if I told you I wasn't discouraged, but I do have confidence in the fact that I'm doing what the Holy Spirit wants me to. The man side of me wants to give up, but the spirit side of me is as strong and defiant as ever in the face of these challenges. The trick is to listen to the spirit side. That's also not the easiest thing to do sometimes, but I try as hard as I can."

Big Jim was wiping grease off of his hands. "Words of wisdom, Max. We'll be there with you every step of the way. Thanks to you guys, I'm back on track and ready to fight the good fight to the end if need be."

"I appreciate that, Jim. We'll be much stronger together. Our prayers will have more power if we're in agreement."

"And agreement it shall be! How about it, Brandon?"

"Right on, Jimbo! Fuel line's all cleaned up and ready to go down here. How about we lay some hands on this beast and see how she runs now that we've given her a good once over?"

"Great! I'll put some gas in the tank and we'll see if the old girl can still run after we've worked on her," laughed Big Jim.

"You boys keep playing mechanic. Joshua and I will see you at the service later tonight."

"See you tonight!" Max wasn't surprised that Big Jim and Brandon answered at the same time.

Big Jim slowly poured fresh gasoline into the tank of the truck. He didn't have any doubts it would run perfectly when they tried to start it up. He had worked on more than a couple of these old trucks and Brandon had a great deal of mechanical skill. With everything all re-wired, lubricated, and adjusted he just knew it would all work and work better than it had before.

"Ready to try it, buddy?"

"Ready and willing, Jimbo."

"Okay, fire it up."

Brandon turned the key. Nothing happened.

"Go ahead, Brandon."

"Uh, Jim, I did. Nothing happened. It's acting like there's no power."

"I thought we went over everything. It's a new battery too."

"I'm not getting any voltage on the gauge in here. There's some sort of problem."

Big Jim started laughing and couldn't stop. Brandon got out of the truck to see what was so funny. Big Jim pointed to the problem and Brandon started laughing too. With all the careful labor they put into the truck, neither of them had remembered to hook the battery up again.

Big Jim finally quit laughing and got a serious look on his face.

"You know brother, this old truck is kind of like us."

"What do you mean?"

"I mean we can have everything in place, everything just right, but we're not going anywhere unless we're hooked into the power source."

"You mean the Holy Spirit?"

"Yep. We better pray for Max right now. He's got a lot going on and our prayers will help."

"You're right, bro. Let's do it."

The two of them leaned on the old truck and prayed their hearts out for Max. It was a strange altar of prayer, but it felt right to them.

"You know," said Big Jim, "that was definitely the right thing to do, because I really feel a whole lot better now."

"So do I," said Brandon, "now hook up that battery so we can see what we've got here."

Big Jim hooked up the battery in no time and the old truck roared to life almost at the instant Brandon turned the switch. The two exchanged looks of satisfaction before Brandon shut the engine off.

"Purrs like a kitten, bro. Just like she ought to," said Brandon.

"You ever hear such a sweet sound?"

"Nope, we have a certified, mechanical orchestra going on here!

"We certainly do. Hey, I think I'm going to drive over to Mr. Korreck's store and show him our handiwork. Want to come along?"

"You go ahead. I think I'm going to try and catch up with Pop and get a little fishing in. I'll see you at the service tonight."

"Yeah, I'll be there. See you, Brandon."

Big Jim was pretty pleased with how the old truck was running. He was hoping that Mr. Korreck would be happy to see how well it worked out for him too. It wouldn't take long to find out because as Big Jim pulled into the driveway, he could see Mr. Korreck was sitting on the bench out in front of the store. It made him feel good to see the big smile on Mr. Korreck's face as he pulled to a stop and got out.

"Hey Jim, looks like you have the old truck running pretty smooth."

"Yeah, my friends gave me a hand on it. We tuned it all up, replaced some of the wiring, and cleaned and lubricated everything. They sure don't make 'em this good anymore. Since your dad took such good care of the truck it was actually pretty easy to fix it up."

"Yeah, he really loved that old truck. He had lots of good memories that revolved around it. It really makes me feel good to see it being used again."

"I can't thank you enough for letting me have it Mr. Korreck."

"Bob, you big ninny. I was actually hoping you'd be coming by. I wanted to talk to you about something."

"Really? What?"

"Remember our last conversation?"

"Well, not really."

"You were talking about God and grace and praying and stuff. I think I'm ready to talk to Max about this stuff and figure it out. I'm beginning to realize that's what has made such a big difference in your life. I'm still not sure I trust some of those church people, but what you have seems to be real and I want in on it."

"Are you sure? Are you really sure you want to do this?"

"Yes. I'm sure."

"That's great! If you're ready, I was going over to the church when I leave here. You can come along."

"But I don't have a suit to wear yet."

"Max never worries about those things. He just says to wear good clothes you already have so you can come to God as you are. He told me people can get too hung up on silly little things like what people wear. He said God will let you know if you need to dress better through something Max calls 'conviction.' I'm not quite sure what that is, but he says I'll understand if I get it."

"Yeah. Hung up like those church people I've always told you about. Max's church must be different."

"It's really all I know, so I can't say much about that. I do know I feel comfortable there, but lately people have been saying I shouldn't be in a church dressed like I am."

"Yeah, I've overheard some of that in the store. People like that have kept me out of church. They seem to think they're better than everyone else."

"It's not like that at Max's church. It's all about Jesus, what He did for us, and God's grace."

"I think I'm going to like it there."

"I think you will too. I have to warn you though, not too many people have been attending lately. I'm afraid it's because of me."

"Well, if they don't want to be around you, then I don't want to be around them. I think we'll do quite nicely without them."

"Mr. Ko….uh, Bob, I don't know if that's the proper Christian attitude, but I do like how you think," laughed Big Jim. "Let's go, your chariot awaits!"

The two of them got in the old truck and got ready to drive to the church. Just like before, the truck roared to life with no effort.

"You sure do have her running like a top, Jim, dad would be proud."

"I'm glad you think so. I can't say enough about how blessed I feel since you gave me this truck."

"I'll tell you a secret Jim. It makes me feel pretty good too."

It was a short ride to church and it seemed like they were there in no time. The two of them hadn't said too much on the ride to the church, mostly just talking about the old truck and plans for fixing it up further.

"We're here, Bob. Time to get the party started!"

"So we are, Jim, so we are. It's been a long, long time since I set foot in a church."

"I don't think the roof is going to collapse when you go inside, Bob, so you can stop worrying about it," laughed Big Jim.

That made Bob laugh. "I think you're right, Jim. Hey, is that Max up there at the door waiting for us?"

"That's Max all right, but I doubt he's there just for us. Probably just greeting the folks as they come in."

Max called out to them as they approached. "Hey Jim, I see you brought some backup!"

"Yep, you remember Bob Korreck, don't you?"

"I certainly do. Welcome Bob."

"Bob's here to talk to you about grace and stuff."

"Sure thing, Bob. I don't have all the answers, but I'll do my best to answer your questions."

"Thanks, Max. I appreciate it."

"We may have plenty of time for your questions too. There's hardly anyone here."

"I've been overhearing comments about that down at the store. It's better to go down the tubes and be right than it is to keep on going and be wrong."

"Those are pretty good words of wisdom, Bob," said Max, "maybe you should be giving the message tonight."

"Nope. I know you're kidding, but I seriously want to learn about this Jesus guy that Jim keeps talking about. It's been a long time since I've been in a church, but I don't remember hearing much about him there other than Christmas and Easter."

"Well, you've come to the right place then. I teach and talk about Jesus as much as I can."

"Great. We'll find some seats and sit down so you can get this started."

The service went along pretty quickly. Other than Big Jim, Brandon, Pop and Bob Korreck, there were only a few other people in attendance that weren't members of Max's family. Max was really happy to see that Bob Korreck was there tonight. The whole reason he had become a pastor was to lead people to Jesus and he was actually excited about talking with Bob after things were over. A little victory like this went a long way in helping him deal with the disappointment of his declining attendance. Bob seemed to be hanging on every word of the message, taking it all in. That was a good sign to Max that he was serious about why he showed up tonight. As everything wrapped up, Bob and Big Jim were still hanging around, waiting to speak with Max.

"Well, pastor, that was quite a speech. I really enjoyed it," said Bob.

"I'm glad you did. It usually flows pretty easily when I talk about the love of Christ."

"That's what I liked. I liked hearing how Jesus loves us and takes care of us. My impression of church life is hearing how bad we are and all the rules we have to follow."

"There are rules, but love is above all that. You don't feel the weight of any legalistic rules when you love Jesus. Some people say that God gave us all those rules and laws to follow to prove to us we aren't capable of following them all. That's why God sent us Jesus. None of us can measure up to God's perfection and Jesus paid the price so that we don't have to. He covered our sins with his blood."

Big Jim laughed. "Hey Bob, Max is just getting warmed up, would you like me to go get you something to eat because it sounds like you might be here for quite a spell."

"Hey!" Max poked a playful punch at Big Jim.

Bob laughed. "I don't mind hearing what he has to say Jim, if you don't mind waiting on me."

"Tell you what Bob," said Max, "how about we let Jim go about his way and I'll take you home when we're through? That way we can take as much time as we need."

"I'm okay with that. How about you Jim?"

"Sure. That will give me some time to cruise around town in the old truck. It's about time I took it out on a pleasure cruise."

"Great, then it's all set. See you later, Jim."

"Yeah, I'll be seeing you guys later."

Big Jim had a big smile on his face as he pulled away from the church in the old truck. It really touched his heart to have Bob in church tonight. He knew that Max would be able to answer any of Bob's questions and explain things in a way that would be easy to understand. In Jim's mind, this would make up for some of the trouble his presence had caused his two friends. He was pretty pleased how the old truck was running too. He had never expected that it would run so smoothly or feel so good to drive. Sure, it was nothing like a modern truck, but it was sure a more pleasurable driving experience with the mechanical feel it provided with the road, something a modern vehicle didn't have. He was just about ready to head back home when he drove past the Brethren Friendship church and saw something that gave him a bad feeling clear down to the pit of his stomach. There behind the bushes in back of the church was a parked motorcycle. A motorcycle with the familiar bloody skull airbrushed on the tank. There was no doubt in Big Jim's mind that this could only be trouble. There was a light on inside the church, so big Jim shut off the engine of the old truck and coasted it to a stop as quietly as he could. He carefully closed the door to the truck, making sure not to make any noise, and crept up to the front door of the church, entering as silently as a man his size possibly could. The inner doors to the sanctuary were open so Big Jim could see inside and his worst fears were confirmed. He could see Pastor Herbert Messner there shaking and clutching an offering plate full of money. He could also see Dwain facing Pastor Messner with a gun aimed right at him.

"Please, you don't have to do this. This is the Lord's money. Just go, I won't tell anyone about this," pleaded Pastor Messner.

"Well the Lord gives and the Lord takes away, and the money is about to be taken from you and given to me," hissed Dwain.

Just seeing this going on made Big Jim's blood start to boil.

"Dwain!"

"Well, well, if it isn't Jimbo. Decide to join me after all? I'll soon have some cash here to start us on our way."

"No Dwain. I told you before, I'm not that guy any more. Now let Pastor Messner be and get out of here."

Big Jim could see the fear in every inch of Pastor Messner's body. He could tell the old man had never had to face anything like this before. He didn't have any plan of action just yet, but he thought it best if he slowly worked his way into a position between Dwain and the pastor. With any luck, Dwain might listen to reason, but he wasn't going to bet on it.

"If you're not going to join me Dunning, just go away. This old man's nothing to you."

"You're wrong there, Dwain. That old man is my brother in the Lord and what you're doing is wrong."

"If that's the way you want this to play out, so be it. But if you don't' want anyone hurt, just get out of the way, okay?"

"No, Dwain. You need to leave."

"No can do, Jimbo. I need that money to finance my run."

"I'm warning you Dwain…."

"Warning me? Who's holding the gun, Jimbo? You tell me that. What's happened to you anyway? You're like a different person."

"It's because I am a different person, Dwain." Big Jim took a step forwards.

"I'm warning you this time, Jimbo. Don't make another move or the old man gets it, understand?" Dwain took two steps so he'd have a clear shot at Pastor Messner.

"Don't do it, Dwain."

"You've been with me before, Jimbo. You know I don't back down. You also know I'm pretty handy with a pistol. One more move and the old man gets it, right between the eyes. Then the next bullet will be for you."

Max was settling down into bed for a good night's sleep. It had been a long time since he had been around anyone as thirsty for knowledge as Bob Korreck had been. It felt good to answer all of Bob's questions and even better to lead him in the sinner's prayer. Whatever Bob had been before, he was now a brother. Max was just about to nod off when he heard the familiar pitter-patter of small feet in the hallway.

"Daddy?"

"Yes, Mary?"

"Daddy, we need to pray for Mister Jim right now, it's important."

"Okay, sweetie, if it's important to you, it's important to me. Come on in and we'll pray."

"Hurry, daddy, it's very important to Mister Jim, he really needs Jesus to help him now."

Max was taken aback by the urgency in Mary's voice, he'd never seen her act this way before and it scared him a little bit. The phone rang as he and Mary knelt in prayer beside the bed. Emma got up out of the bed and went to answer the hall phone so their prayer wouldn't be disturbed. Max could hear her muffled voice in the hallway, but couldn't make out any of the words. She returned just as Mary said "amen."

"Okay, sweetie, that was a good prayer, but now you have to get back to bed. Now scoot!" said Emma.

"Okay, mommy. Maybe you should pray for Mister Jim too."

"I will sweetie. Now get to bed, I need to talk to daddy."

"Okay, mommy, good night!"

"Good night, sweetie."

The smile faded from Emma's face as soon as Mary left the room. Max could tell it was something serious.

"Max, you have to get to the hospital right away. Jim's been shot."

17
A TENSE SCENE

The whole ride to the hospital was just a blur to Max. He couldn't even begin to imagine what had happened because it was unheard of for anyone to get shot in this town. It just didn't happen here. Yet it did. There were several police cars parked around the emergency entrance at the hospital so that told him it was serious. A big part of him was afraid to go inside, so he said a quick prayer for Big Jim and for courage, took a deep breath, and went inside. This whole thing just didn't seem right, like he was watching it all on a movie screen instead of living it. Off to the side of the admissions desk was a group of police officers. What he saw next made his head swim. The officers were surrounding a lone figure, and that lone figure was Pastor Herbert Messner. He knew that Pastor Messner and Big Jim had a past history, but certainly Herbert couldn't have shot Big Jim. No, that couldn't be the case or the police would be taking him out of there and it looked like a couple of them were trying to console him. Max hoped some of this would make more sense soon. As he got closer, he could hear that Pastor Messner was openly sobbing and see that his shirt was covered with blood. Maybe he had shot Jim after all. It was time to quit jumping to conclusions and find out some facts. He was close enough to hear everything now, so it was time for the story to unfold.

"Why? Why?" Pastor Messner got out between sobs. "For me. For me. Why? All this for me."

"Officer? Excuse me, officer?" Max had to get to the bottom of this. "I'm Pastor Maxwell Carson, could you please tell me what's going on?"

"Ah, you're Pastor Carson, we've been expecting you. I'm afraid I have some bad news about your friend James Dunning."

The severity of the situation suddenly hit Max and he leaned against a chair to steady himself. He needed to hear this news, yet he didn't want to hear it.

"Your friend, Mr. Dunning, has been shot and seriously wounded."

"Seriously wounded? So he's still alive then?"

"Yes, I'm sorry, I should have told you he was alive first. His wounds are serious and life threatening though. He may not make it."

Max felt his knees buckling a little so he sat down on the chair.

"Can you tell me what happened?"

"As near as we can tell, Mr. Dunning walked in on a burglary in progress. The suspect fled the scene on a motorcycle. Pastor Messner, here, called 9-1-1. If he hadn't acted so fast and put some direct pressure on the wound, your friend probably wouldn't have made it. Messner's in a bit of shock and we haven't been able to get any more out of him yet. He's mostly just been babbling."

"Higgins."

"Higgins, Pastor Carson?"

"Jim told us the other day about an old acquaintance of his that was in town. Dwain Higgins. He said Higgins was nothing but trouble."

"He saved me. For no reason." Pastor Messner had started talking again.

"Easy, Pastor Messner, you've been through a lot. Just take your time." The officer was trying his best to soothe Pastor Messner's obviously frail mental state. "Pastor Carson's here now, maybe you'd like to talk to him."

Pastor Messner's eyes rose slowly to meet Max's. Max had never seen such a look on anyone's face before. It was a look of total terror mixed with amazement and shock.

"He saved me, Brother Carson, your friend saved me. Why would he do that? Why would he save me?"

"Easy, Brother Messner. Take a deep breath and talk slowly."

"That man. That horrible, horrible man. There was murder in his eyes. He was going to kill me. He pulled the trigger, said he was going to shoot me right between the eyes. Your friend Dunning stepped in the way and took the bullet meant for me and punched that man at the same time. He did it for me. I should be dead."

"What did the man do then?"

"He must have been afraid, because your friend was still standing. I thought he was going to punch him again, but the man got up and ran away. He didn't even grab any of the money, just got up and ran. He was just going out the door when your friend dropped over and I saw the gunshot wound. Why would he do such a thing for me? Why?"

"Because he thought it was the right thing to do, Brother Messner. He thought it was the right thing to do."

"Max! I was hoping you'd show up!"

Max turned to see his old friend, Dr. Torres. "Doc, what's going on? How's Jim?"

"It's not good, Max. Not good at all. Jim's lost a lot of blood. The bullet's done a lot of damage. One good stroke of luck is going in his favor though. My old college buddy, Dr. Bergey, was in town paying me a visit. He just happens to be one of the best vascular surgeons in the country and he's doing the surgery. If he hadn't been here, it would have been a lost cause from the beginning."

"I don't think luck had anything to do with it Doc. I'll make some phone calls and then head back to the chapel for some intense prayer."

"And I'll keep checking in on the surgery and reporting back to you."

"Thanks, Doc."

Brandon and Pop Dunning showed up soon after receiving the phone call from Max. They could see from the grim look on his face that things weren't good.

"How is he Max?" asked Pop.

"I won't lie to you guys. It doesn't look good. Dr. Torres told me the only reason he's alive now is because one of his hot-shot surgeon friends was in town visiting."

"Wow," said Brandon, "what are the odds of that? That's a sure-fire indication of God's providence in action here. That tells me everything's going to work out. We have to believe that."

"Yes we do, Brandon," replied Pop, "but we still need to pray too."

"The faith you guys have is simply amazing," said Max.

"Jimmy was our big prayer warrior. The enemy got him down sometimes, but he always got back up, never accepted defeat. Now that he's the one needing the prayers, we should have the same attitude. We're not giving up. Jimmy wouldn't let us give up."

"And we won't give up, will we?" replied Max.

"No we won't," said Brandon, "we're seeing this thing through till Jim's better."

The three of them went down the hallway to the hospital chapel and made themselves comfortable. They knew if they were to pray like they'd never prayed before they'd have to be able to concentrate on the prayers and not be distracted by the aches and pains of the positions they were in. That comfort was apparent to Dr. Torres when he showed up several hours later to give them an update. All three valiant prayer warriors were fast asleep.

"Uh, hello? Guys?"

"Huh? What?" Max was startled a bit when Dr. Torres woke them up, because he didn't even realize that he had fallen asleep. Pop Dunning woke up by jumping to his feet without even realizing what was going on. Brandon just calmly rose from the altar and acted like he had been awake all along.

"I swear I've never seen folks as calm under pressure as you guys," laughed Dr. Torres.

"Doc, am I right in assuming that your laughter is a sign you have good news for us?" asked Max.

"Jim's not out of the woods just yet, Max, but he is stabilized now. The next few days will be very critical."

"Do you think he will make a complete recovery?" asked Brandon.

"I think there are two factors that will ensure he does. One is his physical condition, the other is the faith of the prayers of you gentlemen. Even if you do fall asleep on the job." Dr. Torres couldn't help but poke a little fun at his friends to keep their mood light.

"Hey, I wasn't asleep," declared Brandon.

"Keep your trap shut, boy," said Pop, "that trail of drool running down the side of your face tells us otherwise."

Brandon's face turned red as they all had a good laugh at his expense.

18
MORE TROUBLE

There were strange sounds bumping around inside his head. Footsteps scurrying around. The sounds of the shoes squeaking occasionally. Some sort of buzzing noises. Equipment making beeping sounds. Muffled sounds of people talking. He thought he could hear a TV playing in the distance. His head was starting to focus now and things were starting to make a little sense. It was dark out. No, his eyes were just shut. Slowly his eyes opened. Everything was so blurry. He blinked a couple times to try and bring things into focus. Slowly the fuzzy images started to make sense. When Brandon's face came into focus, it all started to make sense. He was in a hospital. And still very much alive.

"Well, look who decided to come back to the real world," said Brandon as a big smile broke out on his face.

"I figured you might need me to survive." Big Jim spoke very slowly and each word took a noticeable effort to produce.

"Yeah, you're probably right, but at the moment, you need to just be still and take it easy. You've been through a lot."

"It doesn't feel like I'll be getting up and running around just yet."

"You've been shot. It's going to take a while for that big, ugly body to heal.

"Yeah. I remember now. Dwain. The gun. Last thing I remember was Pastor Messner crying over me."

"He's the one that called 9-1-1. Probably saved your life too."

"I'll have to remember to thank him once I get out of this place."

"I don't think you need to rush. You're in pretty bad shape. You've been unconscious for almost two days. You're lucky one of Doc Torres' friends was in town to patch you up. Doc says he's one of the best and it took everything he knew to put you back together again."

"He should've been around for Humpty Dumpty."

"Wow. They said you lost a lot of blood. Why couldn't some of that bad humor have leaked out of you too?"

Big Jim started to laugh a little and it was obvious that it hurt.

"Okay. Cut that laughing stuff out, it looks like it's not good for you."

"Got a feeling that it would hurt to cry too."

"How about you just keep your mouth shut and stare straight ahead while I go get Pop and Max? We've been taking turns sitting here waiting for you to wake up."

"Guess it's your lucky day. Maybe you should buy a lottery ticket too."

"Very funny, big guy. Keep your jokes to yourself until I get back, okay? Or better yet, tell 'em to the nurses so it's all out of your system and we don't have to hear it."

"You'll just have to take your chances skunk-breath."

"Yeah, I love you too, bro. I'll be right back with the rest of the gang."

"You do that."

Pop could tell by the look on Brandon's face that the news was good. Max was exhausted and had dozed off so Pop gave him a nudge to wake him up.

"He's awake now. Acting like he's been drug around behind a pickup truck for a week, but he's alive and awake."

"Well, what are we waiting for? Let's go," exclaimed Pop.

The three of them rushed back down the hall to Big Jim's room. Dr. Torres and Dr. Bergey were in the room attending to Big Jim when they got there. Both of them had very serious looks on their faces as they checked the equipment, the readings, Jim's vital signs. Dr. Bergey was still wearing his serious expression when he walked over to Pop and stuck out his hand.

"Hello, I'm Dr. Bergey, but you can call me Del. You must be Pop Dunning."

Pop returned the gesture and shook his hand. "That's right, Del, that's who I am. What's the verdict on Jimmy?"

"I wish I had more encouraging news to give you, but it's still too early to tell. Jim had some pretty extensive damage inside. It is a good sign that he's still alive, and I give a lot of the credit for that to the prayers that are being said for him. It is a miracle he survived, and we have to be thankful for that. All we can do is continue those prayers and let the healing process continue."

Max stepped up and shook Dr. Bergey's hand next. "Del, I'm Pastor Carson, but you can call me Max."

"Ah, I've heard a lot about you, young man. Dr. Torres has told me you're a great man of faith."

"I don't know about that, but I try my best. I want to thank you for all you did for Jim. It was truly a blessing that you were here to help."

"Well, the Lord works in mysterious ways."

"You're a Christian, then?"

"Yes, Dr. Torres and I became friends in college, and recently we got together at a Christian retreat for doctors. He told me all about the faithful Pastor Carson and how much he'd learned from him."

Max started to blush a bit as he shot a look to the other side of the room and saw Dr. Torres smiling a big smile at him.

"I'm sure I got in Dr. Torres' way about as much as I helped him learn."

"Don't let him kid you Del, my boy Max is the real deal."

Max was really blushing now. Brandon stepped up to shake Dr. Bergey's hand next.

"I'm Brandon. Thank you for saving my brother."

"Pleased to meet you, young man. Any brother of Jim's must be pretty extraordinary himself."

"I'm nothing special. What I am today is because of these guys here with me in this room. Without them, I'm nothing. You, on the other hand, you have hands that have been blessed by God to do great things."

"I can't deny God has placed a blessing on my life. He saves lives, I get to take some of the credit, and I get to meet nice folks like yourselves. I'm anxious for this big guy in the bed to get better so I can get to know him better too. I've heard the stories, I've held his insides in my hands, and God's touched him. I want to find out why."

"Hey, I hate to break up this party here, but could you guys let me in on it too?"

They all turned to look at Big Jim and saw that he had a big smile on his face.

"Dr. Bergey, you'll excuse me if I don't get up, but are you the guy I have to thank for putting me back together?"

"You better not get up, young man, you need to lay still so you can heal. I spent a lot of time gluing you back together and I don't want it to all fall apart again."

"Fair enough. Thanks for putting me back together doc. I don't think these other clowns could make it without me."

"Well, aren't you the special one?" laughed Brandon.

Big Jim tried to laugh, but the amount of pain he was in kept him from doing it. Dr. Bergey quickly walked over to the monitors that were hooked up to Jim and studied the readouts.

"You need to be careful there, Jim. Just remain calm. Your heart jumped around a bit when you tried to laugh. It's been under a great strain and you need to really, really take it easy."

"I'd salute, but I'm not sure I can raise my arm."

"Well right now, I prescribe complete rest for you. And not only you, but also for Pop, Pastor Max, and Brandon. We've got everything under control here as much as possible and you other folks need to go home and get some rest. It won't do any good if Jim gets better and one of you guys drops over. All three of you guys have practically been living here the last few days."

"You do have a point there, Doc. We probably should all go home, get cleaned up, and get a good night's sleep now that the worst is over," said Pop.

"Yeah, you guys get out of here so an invalid can get some rest."

Big Jim hadn't been awake long, but they all could tell their little visit was a strain for him.

"We'll come back and see you tomorrow after you had your beauty sleep," said Brandon. "On second thought, a beauty coma wouldn't make a dent in that big of a stack of ugly."

"I'm going to smack you right up alongside your head as soon as I get better," said Big Jim.

Big Jim was getting so weak he could barely get the words out. That was the cue to the others that it was really time to leave.

"We'll be back tomorrow, Jimmy. You take care, now," said Pop.

All Big Jim could do was nod at Pop before he fell asleep.

The sun was shining the next day when Brandon, Pop, Joshua, and Max met at the hospital to see Jim. They had all gotten a good night's sleep, confident in knowing that Big Jim was on the mend and that God was in control of the situation. They each had more spring in their step than they had the day before and they were all feeling refreshed and anxious to see Big Jim again.

"Hold up a second," said Brandon, "there's something I need to do."

The other three looked at each other puzzled as Brandon ran off around the corner of the building. They were just as puzzled when he reappeared holding a handful of freshly picked flowers from the landscaping on the other side of the hospital.

"Don't look so surprised, guys. These flowers will not only help him look better, they'll probably make him smell better too."

Max just shook his head. "You two guys deserve each other. Mostly because no one else would put up with the two of you."

"I'm just praising God that there is still two of us."

"Yes, He is definitely to be praised for this. His hand is evident through the whole ordeal."

"If you two are through flapping your gums, let's get in there and see Jimmy," said Pop.

"Aye, aye, captain," said Brandon playfully as he saluted Pop and disappeared inside the automatic doors, flowers held high.

"Kids," muttered Pop as he shook his head and followed Brandon inside.

Max and Joshua just looked at each other and laughed as they followed the other two inside. It was good to see Brandon and Pop with a familiar spring in their step again.

The last few days of maintaining a vigil in Big Jim's room had taken a toll on both of them, especially Pop, and the comfort of being able to talk to Big Jim allowed them to have a very restful night's sleep. Brandon, Pop, and Joshua went on ahead to Big Jim's room instead of waiting for Max. One of the hazards of Max's visitation trips to the hospital was that he always knew more than a couple of the patients and had to say a few words to them as he passed by. It was almost half an hour later when he finally caught up to the rest of them at the room. When he stepped into Big Jim's room, it was immediately obvious that Brandon and Pop weren't the only ones to benefit from a restful night of sleep. Big Jim was actually sitting up in the bed and he sounded normal instead of the pained voice he had the day before.

"It's about time you showed up. We were beginning to think you got lost," said Big Jim to Max.

"Well, you know how it is. Everyone wants visitors, so I had to oblige a few folks along the way."

"You know what they say, you can take the pastor out of the church, but you can't take the church out of the pastor," laughed Brandon.

"Maybe we should call Dr. Bergey in here and see if he can surgically remove that bad humor," said Max, "there's obviously no cure for it."

"Now look who's trying to be funny. Maybe you should save the wise cracks for your next sermon. It might help keep people awake," laughed Brandon.

"Maybe I should. It would be pretty easy to just follow you around for material."

"Watching you guys is more painful than getting shot."

Max and Brandon both quit talking and turned to see Big Jim looking at both of them with a big smile on his face. Max felt a little ashamed that he was having so much fun that he forgot for a moment why he was here.

"Sorry to cause you more pain, Jim," said Max with a smile, "how are you doing?"

"Other than being shot, unable to move, confined to a hospital room, and forced to eat hospital food, pretty good. Yourself?"

"Hey, never mind how I'm doing. You're the one in the hospital."

"Maybe. But it's going to take more than a scumbag with a gun to keep me here."

"Let's see that you never run across another scumbag with a gun, okay?"

"It wasn't like I went looking for him, you know."

"I know. From what I heard, you got a pretty good punch in on old Dwain. That should've been enough to convince him to stay away from here."

"It's hard to tell. He could be pretty stubborn at times."

"More stubborn than you? I doubt it," laughed Brandon.

"You guys aren't very entertaining," said Jim. "How about we get some news on TV and see what I've missed out on the last couple days."

"Hey look," said Joshua, "isn't that news anchor someone you guys went to school with?"

"Yeah," replied Brandon, "probably another one of those nerds Jim would beat up on."

The scene was interrupted by the sound of Max's phone ringing in his pocket.

"Sorry guys," said Max, "but I better take this call."

Max stepped out in the hall while the others continued to watch the news show on TV. While the anchorman was reading the story about the new trees that were being planted downtown, they could see one of the workers in the studio handing him a note.

"This just in," said the man on the TV screen, "our field reporter is on the scene on what appears to be a possible hostage situation."

"Say," said Pop, "isn't that Max's church on the TV?"

"It is!" exclaimed Joshua, "I wonder what's going on?"

"No!" They heard Max shout from the hallway and he sounded frantic.

"They have Dwain Higgins cornered down at the church. He has Mary. I've got to leave immediately."

Big Jim, Brandon, and Pop could only watch in silence as Max ran out of the hospital.

19
THE STANDOFF

Max was a block away from the church when he was stopped by a police road block. He didn't even bother parking his car, he just hopped out to confront the policeman.

"I'm sorry, sir, you can't go any further. We have a dangerous situation in progress."

"Listen, that is my church and my daughter down there. You will let me go down there, no argument."

"No, sir, I can't allow that."

Max was starting to get impatient. "Listen, I know you're just doing your job, but I need to do my job and be down there and be there for my child."

"I'm sorry, sir."

"Get out of my way before I do something we're both going to regret."

"Take one step further, sir, and I'm afraid I'll have to place you under arrest."

"You're going to what?"

"Is that Pastor Carson?" Chief Norris' voice took both Max and the policeman by surprise. They had been so busy with their interaction they didn't notice that Chief Norris had walked up behind them.

"It's okay, John, this is Pastor Carson and that is his church. He can come with me."

Max was too upset to savor his victory over the policeman, but he did turn and stick his tongue out as he passed by him.

"Stay low, Pastor Carson. The man inside is armed and we don't really know what to expect of him."

"Tell me what's going on Chief. How did this happen?"

"The suspect's name is Dwain Higgins, a real bad apple. From what we've been able to piece together, we believe he came here to steal valuables from your church. He was trying to get back to his motorcycle over there, when one of my men just happened by on patrol and spooked him. Your little girl was playing over there and Higgins grabbed her to use as a hostage. He wants us to let him go and we've been trying to negotiate for the hostage's release."

"And have you had any luck?"

"We're waiting for the SWAT team to show up right now."

"You mean you're planning on shooting it out with him?"

"We hope it doesn't come to that, but it's not looking good. He has a good tactical position in the church. We can't see any way of getting an advantage on him. What is that you're doing?"

"Praying. I'm about out of my mind here, so I have to turn this all over to God or I'm going to flip out."

"While you're at it, make it a good one. We need all the help we can get."

"I can't lose hope. I just can't. I have to believe God will get us through this and get Mary back safely."

"Would you like to try talking to him? I haven't had any luck yet. Maybe your voice would make a difference."

"Okay, if you think it will help."

"I think it's worth a shot." Chief Norris handed Max his bull horn. "Just push that button there and talk into it. He'll be able to hear you loud and clear."

Max couldn't hide his nervousness as he took the bullhorn from Chief Norris. He had never been this scared before in his entire life. This wouldn't be so hard if it were someone else's child in danger. But it wasn't someone else's, it was his own precious Mary.

"Help me, Jesus," Max said quietly as he raised the bullhorn to his lips. "Dwain Higgins, this is Pastor Max Carson. You're in my church and that's my little girl you have with you in there. Let's talk about settling this thing so we can all go on our way in peace."

The voice that came from inside the church sounded agitated. "I hear you, Preacher. What do you have in mind?"

Max didn't have an answer and looked hopefully at Chief Norris, who just motioned silently for Max to keep going.

"Let my daughter go and we'll talk."

"No can do, Preacher-man. As soon as I let her go, I'm a dead man. She stays with me."

"That won't happen. Let's just talk this out."

"She's my trump card, preacher. If anyone makes a move against me, I'll kill her. If anyone tries to come in here after me, I'll kill them too. I'm serious, so don't test me. I'm pretty good with a gun and I've got plenty of ammo here, so no funny business, okay? Just get me a car so I can get out of here and the girl doesn't get hurt."

"I'll see what I can do."

"You do that Preacher. I'm going to give you a little example so you know I mean business. Put that bullhorn down on the hood of that cop car."

Max carefully laid the bullhorn down on the car in front of him. No sooner than his hand had left the handle, a shot rang out from the church and the bullhorn laid at his feet in pieces.

"I don't miss, Preacher-man. Do what you need to do to keep that from happening to anyone you care about."

Max sunk down behind the police car dejected. He couldn't see a way out of this. Unfortunately, neither could Chief Norris at this point.

20
FACING DANGER

Pop and Brandon were watching the news on TV with Big Jim, each of them praying silently and hoping for a bulletin with good news.

"There should be something soon, those police know how to handle these situations," said Brandon.

"Yes," answered Pop, "they'll have this thing wrapped up in no time. Don't look so concerned, Jimmy. It will all be over soon."

"No one around here knows Dwain like I do. He won't give up."

"God has this under control, Jimmy. It won't do you any good to get all worked up, just sit back and heal."

"God better have this under control, because with Dwain in the picture it will take a miracle for it to end well."

"Well, there's nothing He can't do. We just have to have faith, right Brandon?"

"That's right, Pop. He's pulled us through before and he'll do it again. You should know that ugly brother, you're the one that always lectured us on the subject."

"All the evil that's been floating around here makes me wonder, that's all."

"Hey, no wandering around for you until you're better!" laughed Brandon.

"You may be my brother, but that humor is so bad it's not worthy of even a chuckle."

Brandon just laughed and shook his head.

"Hey Jimmy, Bob Korreck wanted me to call with an update on your condition," said Pop. "If you don't mind, I think I'll slip on out to the lounge and give him a call."

"Sure, that's fine. Say, Brandon, I'm feeling like eating a hamburger. Do you think you could run down to the cafeteria and have them cook one up for me while Pop's gone? Maybe you guys would like something too."

"No problem, bro. How about you Pop? Want me to pick something up for you too?"

"No, I think I'll be fine. Thanks anyway. We'll both be back soon, Jimmy."

"Take your time. Don't rush on my account."

Some time had passed when Brandon and Pop met up again outside of Big Jim's room.

"You're missing out, Pop. I got a hamburger for me and Jim both and they really smell good."

"That they do, Brandon. Maybe I should've gotten one. It just makes me happy that Jimmy felt good enough to want one."

"Yeah, me too. Kind of scary seeing him laid up like he is."

The two of them had quite a surprise when they stepped into Big Jim's room. Instead of finding a hungry patient, they found an empty bed. This was not what they expected. The two exchanged questioning glances and Pop walked over to check out the restroom.

"Jimmy?" Pop knocked softly on the door, hoping for an answer. When there was none, he opened up the door slowly, expecting the worst. It was a relief to find the restroom empty, but there was still no answer to the mystery.

"Pop, look here," said Brandon, "this closet is empty and Jim's clothes are gone. Looks like his hospital gown wadded up here in the bottom. You don't suppose….." Brandon's voice tailed off.

"I don't see how the Jim we left behind could've gotten out of bed let alone leave, but it looks like he's gone."

"Maybe if we hurry, we can find him. He surely can't be moving too fast."

Pop got a scared look on his face. "He knows where I keep the spare key to my truck."

"We better try to get to the truck first," exclaimed Brandon.

They ran down the hall and out into the parking lot as fast as they could.

"Uh, say Pop, weren't we parked over there?"

Pop looked to where Brandon was pointing, but there were no empty parking spaces there.

"I thought we were. I hate to say it, but he's been gone long enough that it appears someone's already taken the parking space."

"What do you think we should do now?"

"Well, I guess the first thing we do is give Bob a call and see if he can come over and pick us up. I don't think either of us have to guess too hard to figure out where Jimmy went."

The scene back at the church was still pretty tense. Max and Chief Norris were crouched behind one of the police cars waiting for another opportunity to try to negotiate. Dwain Higgins was not giving in to any of their requests to free Mary or to compromise on any of his demands. Max was becoming very discouraged with the current situation.

"What do you think we should do, Chief Norris?"

"I don't know Max. Right now it seems like our best bet is to just wait. He'll get hungry at some point in time and perhaps he'll give up then."

"But Mary will be hungry too. And scared. Maybe getting cold."

"I'm sorry, Max, but there's nothing we can do about that."

"Max!"

Max heard a familiar voice calling to him and turned to see who it was. He knew it couldn't be Big Jim, because Max knew he was in no condition to be out of his hospital bed, let alone be here. Max did a double take because he couldn't believe his eyes. It was, in fact, Big Jim coming in his direction.

"You know that fellow, Max?" asked Chief Norris.

"Yes. He's a friend of mine. He may be able to help us out because he knows this Higgins character personally."

"If he knows Higgins, are you sure he can be trusted?"

"I'd stake my life on it, Chief."

Chief Norris cast a wary eye on Big Jim as he walked up. He looked much like the character they had cornered in the church only a lot larger and his eyes actually looked a lot meaner.

"Say, I had an officer stationed over there blocking the road. How did you get past him?"

"Sir, I don't mean any disrespect to anyone, but you might want to send a man over to check on him. He got a little aggressive when I wouldn't stop, and I'm afraid I had to punch him."

"You punched him? And then he let you go past?"

"Uh, no, I punched him and he dropped like a rock. Don't worry, I checked and he's still breathing okay."

Chief Norris really wondered about this mountain of a man now. He wasn't about to turn his back on him.

"So how'd you get out of the hospital, Jim?" asked Max.

"Just you never mind about that Max. I'm here to help Mary."

"So you're a friend of Max's?" asked Chief Norris.

"Yes sir," said Big Jim as he stuck out his hand, "name's Dunning, Jim Dunning. What can I do to help?"

"Pleased to meet you Mr. Dunning. I'm afraid there's nothing anyone can do at the moment. Right now we're trying to wait him out. We're still hoping he gives up before the SWAT team shows up and any fireworks take place."

"I know Dwain, sir. He's not the type to give up. He's also not the type to shy away from killing anyone either. I don't see this ending well."

"It's all we can do, Dunning."

"It might be all you can do, Chief. But I came here to make sure nothing happens to Mary. I aim to get her out of there."

"Don't think of doing anything stupid Dunning. There's nothing anyone can do right now."

"You're wrong, Chief. I know Dwain. I don't think there's anyone in this world that could talk him out of anything. Ever. Except maybe me."

"Well Dunning, if you want to try to negotiate, here's a bullhorn. Be careful, he shot the other one."

"You're lucky that's all he shot. I've never known or seen a better shot than Dwain."

"You know what you're up against, then?"

"Yes, I do. But Dwain doesn't know what he's up against yet."

That last remark stunned and puzzled Chief Norris. The more he thought about it the more concerned he became. He also made sure to call someone to check on his officer who was punched out because he was starting to have doubts about his well-being.

"Dwain! It's Jim!" Jim's voice echoed back at them with a force none of them were expecting.

"Jim! I thought I shot you. Did you come to your senses and want to join me after all? I'm off to a rocky start, but we can still pull this off together. Just like old times."

"Just who is this friend of yours?" whispered Chief Norris to Max. Chief Norris was beginning to wonder just which side Big Jim was on.

"Dwain, I'm not here to join you," continued Big Jim, "I'm here to get the little girl. She's a good friend of mine and I don't want her hurt."

"That's a funny one! The great Jim Dunning buddied up with a little girl. I suppose you play with dolls together too, eh?"

"Whenever she wants to," replied Big Jim calmly.

"Go away, Jimbo. She's my ticket out of her. She's coming with me."

"No Dwain. I'm giving you a choice. Either you let her go, or I'm coming to get you."

"I've got a gun, Jimbo. You know that. If I shot you once, you know I'll do it again."

"Ten seconds, Dwain. If you don't send her out, I'm coming in after her."

"Suit yourself. I'll be waiting."

"Jim, you can't do this. He'll shoot you. What if he hurts Mary?" asked Max, the fear in his voice evident.

Chief Norris spoke up. "He's right, Dunning. Higgins is too dangerous to deal with alone."

"Well Chief, if he's as dangerous as you think, I won't make it far. And Max, I figure there's a greater chance of Mary getting hurt if a SWAT team shows up."

"Dunning, I can't let you take the risk," said Chief Norris.

"I'm sorry you feel that way Chief. Since you won't let me, you should know I'm just going to do it anyway."

"Max, talk some sense into your friend."

"There's no talking to him when his mind is made up Chief. And I think he has a point about Mary getting hurt."

"Don't do it, Dunning."

Big Jim turned his attention away from Max and Chief Norris and looked towards the church. Before Chief

Norris could say another word, Big Jim laid down the bullhorn and started walking toward the church. He didn't make it five feet before a shot rang out making the dirt fly at Big Jim's feet.

"It will take more than that to stop me Dwain."

"That was just a warning shot, Jimbo. I owed you that one. You won't be so lucky with the next shot."

"I'm still coming Dwain."

Big Jim kept walking towards the church. Every few steps was met with a gunshot and more dirt flying up, but Big Jim never changed his pace. Chief Norris and Max both cringed with each shot, expecting to see Big Jim drop each time. It seemed like it took an eternity for Big Jim to reach the church door, but it was only seconds in reality. They both watched nervously as they saw him go inside.

When Big Jim stepped inside, he immediately saw Dwain backed into the corner of the room, holding Mary with the gun pointed at her head. Even with all the gunshots and the danger of the situation, Mary got a big smile on her face when she saw Big Jim. That smile always made him feel good inside and he hoped it wouldn't be the last time he saw it.

"Back off, Jim. I'll do it! I'll do it!"

"Let her go," Big Jim replied calmly. "Let her go or you'll have to deal with me. Do it now!"

At that moment, Big Jim saw a change in Dwain. His cold, steely eyes were now wide open and growing wider by the second. The expression on his face was one of complete terror. He was no longer looking Big Jim in the eye, but seemed to be focused on something else.

"Let her go." This time Jim's voice was much more forceful. What happened next was such a blur that Big Jim wasn't quite sure just how it all took place. Dwain let go of Mary and she ran straight to Big Jim and jumped in his arms. At the same time, Dwain started shooting, but none of the shots seemed to be anywhere near either of them.

Max gasped in horror when the shots started to ring out. Chief Norris feared the worst and motioned for his officers to move in. What they saw next caused them all to stop in their tracks dumbfounded. Emerging from the church door was Big Jim and he was carrying Mary, who was not only not scared, but appeared to be laughing. They could still hear some shooting coming from the church, but Big Jim just walked towards them carrying Mary as if nothing else was happening. As they got to the police car, Big Jim let Mary down so she could run to Max. The shots stopped inside the church at about the same time. Without even making a demand, Dwain's gun came flying out the church door. The officers carefully crept to the door, weapons at the ready, only to find Dwain Higgins, cowering in a corner.

Max was holding Mary tightly, "sweetie, I was so afraid for you. I'm so glad you're okay."

"I was always okay, daddy. I knew Jesus was with me all the time and I always knew Mister Jim would come get me."

There was a lot of talking going on all at once, but the sounds were starting to sound muffled to Big Jim's ears. He looked around a little bit and it felt like he was starting to see things that were far, far away up close. He was also starting to have a sense of being able to see through buildings and hear people talking miles away. He wasn't sure what was going on, but the pain from his gunshot had gone away. It felt like he was starting to float. That was the last sensation he felt before he dropped over.

Chief Norris spoke up, "I've got to hand it to you, Dunning, you sure came through. Dunning?"

They all turned to find Big Jim lying face down on the ground.

"Somebody call an ambulance," screamed Max.

21
DWAIN'S STORY

The room was full of the mechanical and electrical sounds of medical machinery. There were so many machines and tubes around that most people wouldn't recognize the body in the bed as being that of Big Jim Dunning. Max had not left Big Jim's side since the nurses wheeled his gurney into the room after his surgery was over. He was completely exhausted from being in prayer outside the operating room for the entire 12 hours of surgery, plus the six hours since Big Jim had been brought back. He knew he wasn't responsible for Big Jim being here, but he was so moved by Big Jim's sacrifice to save Mary that he felt it was his responsibility to pray continually until Jim got better.

Dr. Bergey entered the room to check up on Big Jim and saw Max praying over him. "Max, you need to get some rest. There's no way you can keep on going like this."

"I need to do this until he's okay, doc."

"Max. You have to face the facts. He might not make it this time. It took a miracle to keep him alive before and it's beyond me how he summoned up the strength to leave here, let alone save Mary like he did. He was barely alive after he was first shot and now I can't give you a single good reason why he's still here with us. From what I hear, it was a miracle that none of those bullets hit him, but I wouldn't expect another miracle. I did my best to put back together everything that came apart again, but there was so much more damage inside this time with all the twisting and tearing. I'm sorry to say it, but I don't have great confidence he'll pull through."

"I'm sorry doc. I have to believe he will. I just have to."

"And I just have to believe right along with you, Max." Max turned around to see that Bob Korreck had stuck his head in the room.

"You need your rest Max. I'll take a shift and watch over Jim. Brandon and Pop will take turns too. Don't try to carry the load all by yourself, you'll just crumble. I won't take no for an answer."

"You're probably right, Bob, but I can't help it. Jim sacrificed himself to save Mary. I feel like I owe him."

"Jim didn't do it for you to owe him, he did it because he cared about Mary. I'm sure if he was given the choice, he'd do it again too. Now get over this and get out of here for a while. If there's any change I'll let you know."

"You make quite an argument, Bob. I should probably check in with Brandon and Pop anyway."

"You do that, Max. After you go home and get some sleep. I'll hold down the fort here."

"Okay. I'll see you later, Bob. Take good care of him, okay?"

"That's what the doctors are here for. I'll just watch him and pray the best I can. See you, Max."

Max was shocked when he woke up the next morning. He knew he was tired when he went to bed, but sleeping till almost noon was something he hadn't done since he pulled all-nighters back in college. It was definitely the peace of the Holy Spirit that let him rest so well. He was still working on waking up when he walked out into the kitchen where his wife, Emma, was making lunch. He was surprised to see Pop and Brandon were there too, sitting at the kitchen table.

"Well, if it isn't Sleeping Beauty," Emma chuckled.

"Yeah, I know. Why didn't you wake me?"

"You needed your rest, sweetie. You've barely slept since Jim was first shot. How is he, by the way?"

"The doctor doesn't have much hope."

Emma gasped, "no!"

"I'm still believing for a miracle. You should too. Hey, Pop, what brings you and Brandon here?"

"We knew there wasn't anything we could do for Jimmy right now, so we thought we'd check up on you. You've been through a lot lately, and frankly, we're both a little worried about you."

"And we had a question for you too," added Brandon.

"You guys don't need to worry about me, I'm fine."

"You do look kind of stressed though, even if you did just get out of bed," said Pop.

"I said, I'll be fine. Now what's this about a question? What do you want to know?"

Pop and Brandon exchanged a glance at each other before Brandon spoke.

"We were thinking about what happened over at the church and there's something we don't understand. We thought maybe since you were there, you could shine a little light on it."

"Okay, what is it?"

"We heard Higgins was a crack shot."

"I'll say. He shot the bullhorn right off the car when I sat it down."

"Well then, if he was so good, how come all of those shots he fired at Jim missed? We heard he pretty much emptied his gun."

Max just stood there, stunned. In all the excitement, he hadn't really thought of that before and they were absolutely right. How could such a good shot miss such a huge target as Jim?

"I have to say I don't know. I guess we'll have to give the praise to the Lord for that one."

"Yeah, that's all we could come up with too. Do you think it was some kind of miracle?"

"All I know for sure is that Jim is still with us by the grace of God and I believe that grace will keep him with us."

"Amen," said Pop and Brandon together.

The whole time the four of them sat at the table, Max couldn't get the question out of his head. Just how had Higgins missed Jim all those times? It didn't make any sense at all. And why did Higgins give himself up so easily at the end? He went from being ready to go out in a blaze of gunfire to being a timid creature in a corner. What brought about all this? Max didn't have an answer, but he knew he wouldn't be able to rest until he found out more. He couldn't think of a better place to start, than right at the source, Dwain Higgins. At least he would be easy to find. All Max had to do was drive down to the county jail to find him. It wasn't like Higgins would be able to hide. As he looked outside at Mary playing with her dolls, he wondered if he would be able to face Higgins, the man who just a day earlier had threatened to kill her. Would he be blinded by anger or would he be able to find the grace to forgive him? Those thoughts were interrupted as he passed by Mary on his way to the car.

"Come play tea party with me, daddy!"

"I'm on my way to go talk to someone, sweetie, but I can stop long enough for one sip."

"You can sit there, beside Ann."

"Okay, sweetie. Why's there a cup there with no one sitting at it? All the other dolls have cups."

"That's Mister Jim's place. Ann and me thought we'd keep a cup ready for Mister Jim till he comes back. We like playing tea party with Mister Jim."

Max felt his eyes getting a little watery. "Sweetie, you know Mister Jim is in the hospital don't you? Sometimes people don't come home from the hospital, sometimes they go home to be with Jesus instead."

"I know that daddy. Jesus told me Mister Jim was going to come back and play tea party some more."

"Oh. Okay." Max didn't have any kind of answer for that.

Thinking about Mary leaving a place for Jim and thinking of how none of those bullets had hit Jim kept Max's mind occupied during the whole drive down to the jail. This whole thing was just so bizarre. Maybe there was some sort of miracle in the making here and he was going to be a part of it. That had to be it. The bullets had to be some sort of miracle. All he had to do was get Dwain's side of the story to confirm it. The doctors thought it was a miracle that Jim was still alive. Either God was working in all of this or Max was going to be tremendously disappointed. That thought made him focus more. He knew disappointment came from the enemy. He had to keep believing and have faith that God was going to handle it, no matter what the outcome.

Max said a quick prayer as he pulled into the parking lot of the jail. "Lord, help lead me here, I can't see the path you want us to follow. Let me know it's you."

Max was always a little hesitant when he walked up the sidewalk to the jail to visit someone, and this time was no different. No matter how hard the government had worked to make the jail building look professional, it always had an air of cold institutionalism about it. The glass security doors out front were always nice and clean, but they had an air of control to them to when they closed shut behind him. The lobby was clean, with modern furniture, but the melancholy mood of the people there to see their loved ones took all the cheeriness out of the room the government tried to put into it. He now came to the part that annoyed him more than anything else that happened within these walls. No matter how hard he worked to put on a cheerful face and attitude, the person manning the visitor's station always remained completely emotionless. This time was no different.

"Name." The voice couldn't be any more cold or void of emotion.

"Carson, Pastor Maxwell Carson."

"Who are you here for?"

"Higgins, Dwain Higgins."

"Sign here and walk over to that gentlemen over there."

The next guy was just as emotionless as the first.

"Walk through the metal detector, please."

Max knew all about this step of the visit, so he had removed any offending metals from his pocket before he had come inside to make it go more smoothly.

"You're clear. Press the button over there and they'll buzz you through the door."

Inside the door was a very thick sheet of bullet-proof glass with phone banks on either side for people on each side to talk into. Max took a seat near the middle of the row of chairs and waited for Higgins to be brought out. It wasn't much of a wait because one of the guards brought Higgins out right away. He didn't look as mean in his orange jump suit as he had when Max last saw him at the church, but he was every bit as evil-looking, this time with a difference. Now his eyes had more of a look of fear and he was looking around like he was afraid of being stalked. Max wasn't sure, but it looked like Dwain recognized him as he sat down and picked up his phone.

"You're that preacher guy, aren't you? The father of the little girl I took?"

"Yes, that's me."

"She okay? What about Dunning? "

"Yes, she's fine. She actually handled it better than the rest of us did. Jim, on the other hand is not in good shape. The doctors say he doesn't have much chance of pulling through because of all the damage that was done the first time you shot him. Do you mind if I ask you a few questions Mr. Higgins?"

"Go ahead."

"I understand you're something of a marksman and you demonstrated it on that day. How come you couldn't hit your target when you fired at Jim?"

Higgins suddenly appeared agitated with that question, like he was nervous and scared. He looked around the room several times before he answered in a whisper.

"I'm not sure. Every shot I took should have hit him. I have an idea what happened, but I don't believe it myself."

"An idea?"

"Yeah. Dunning's a pretty big dude, right?"

"Yes."

"Well, he's the biggest guy I've ever known. Biggest dude I've ever seen. Until that day."

"I don't understand. I was there. I think I would've remembered seeing someone else that big."

"Well he was there. Dressed all in white. He came in the door right behind Dunning, but when I aimed the gun, he stepped in front. So big I couldn't even see Dunning any more. I tried shooting him first, but ….."

"But what?"

"This part can't be real, it just can't. I had to imagine it, some sort of hallucination. Maybe a drug flashback, I don't know."

"Easy, now, easy, just tell me what happened."

"When I started shooting, the big guy……."

"Go on. Please."

"He pulled out a big sword and swatted the bullets away like I was pitching a softball at him underhanded. Can't be real, I had to imagine it, right? Right?"

Max sat there stunned for a few seconds before he could answer.

"I think what you saw was real. I think it was an angel."

"An angel? Those things aren't real are they?"

"I've never seen one, but I've always believed in them and I know they exist. What you're telling me now just proves it for sure."

"And you think this angel was protecting Dunning and the girl?"

"Apparently so. Hey, it looks like my time is up. I'll have to be going."

"Wait, Preacher, don't go yet. I've been a bad man most of my life. Dunning was every bit as bad as me. I already shot him once. He knows I would've killed him, yet he was willing to give his life to save the girl. He's changed. He's changed and now he's got that…that thing watching over him. Can you tell me what made the change in him? I'd like to have some of whatever it is and change too. Can we talk about it some more?"

"Dwain, the big change in Jim came when he gave his life over to Jesus Christ and made Him his savior. Would you like to accept Jesus as your savior?"

"I'd always thought that Jesus stuff was just for losers. Dunning's never been a loser, so I'm willing to give it a try."

"Okay, Dwain, we'll have to make this quick. I'm going to lead you in a prayer called the Sinner's Prayer and you have to repeat it after me and mean every word of it. If you fake any of it, we're just wasting our time."

"Let's do it, preacher."

Max went through the sinner's prayer faster than he ever had before and Dwain repeated every word. Max had doubts if he really meant it, but he thought he saw tears forming in Dwain's eyes when they were through.

"I have to go now, Dwain. Talk to the chaplain here and I'll come back. Promise."

Dwain nodded and hung up the phone.

22
FORGIVENESS

Max left the jail with mixed emotions. He was excited to tell everyone about the angel, happy that Dwain Higgins had made a decision to follow Jesus, yet still concerned about Big Jim. The doctor gave him little to hope for and all the tubes running into Big Jim made it seem like the machinery was all that was keeping him alive. Even though the situation seemed hopeless, there was still the matter of the angel. Would God have sent an angel to protect Big Jim if He didn't have more work for Jim to do? And where was that angel the first time Jim was shot? This was just one of those mysterious ways the Lord worked in, but it sure wasn't easy trying to wait till the mystery was revealed. He'd have the entire night to ponder that before the group met at the hospital the next morning to pray over Jim. He didn't really want to spend the whole night thinking about it, but restful sleep refused to come to him that night. Every time he would start to doze off, another dream of Jim, Dwain, Mary, and angels would wake him up. He was so tired when he did drag himself out of bed the next morning that it was all he could do to gather up the strength to get ready and go to the hospital. He wasn't sure he would have enough strength after that for the morning service, but he'd figure out how to get through that when the time for it came. If only he had a fraction of the energy Mary had.

"Come on daddy, let's go. I want to see Mister Jim."

"Sweetie, you know we talked about this and decided it would be best if you didn't see him."

"No, daddy. You decided I wouldn't see him."

"And you will obey me. No more discussion."

Mary stomped her foot and gave Max an angry glare, but she didn't argue. It was obvious though, that she was still very angry when Emma loaded her into the car.

"I'm a little scared about seeing Jim, honey," said Emma.

"Why's that?"

"What if he doesn't make it? Don't you worry about it yourself?"

"The worst thing that could happen is that he doesn't' make it and then he'll be with Jesus. That's not so bad is it? Besides, I have something to spring on everyone that should change how we look at it all."

"Really? What's that?"

"We're almost there. I'll let everyone in on it at the same time so I only have to tell the tale once."

"Sounds intriguing."

"Oh, it is. It is."

When Max pulled into the hospital parking lot, he could see that everyone was already there. He parked right beside Pop Dunning's truck and he could see Bob Korreck's truck was in the next row over. If anything could bring Big Jim back, it would be the power of their prayers. He was hoping the story of Higgins and the angel would give the group an extra boost of intensity. There was a quiet air about the place as they entered into the front lobby of the hospital. It seemed almost too quiet.

They could see the others gathered outside Big Jim's room as they started down the hallway.

"Hey everybody, are we ready to get started?" asked Max.

"Max, before we start, I should tell you the doctor was here a few minutes ago. He said it's still not looking good," said Pop.

Max could see Joshua turn his head so no one could see the tears starting down his cheeks. Brandon put his hand on Joshua's shoulder for reassurance. Bob Korreck was just taking it all in, not sure what to think.

"I know it looks bad," started Max, "but we can't be wandering around defeated. Jim wouldn't let us act this way if he could speak to us. We can't let him down. We can't let God down. We have to believe for more than what things appear to be. Especially after the talk I had with Dwain Higgins yesterday."

"Higgins?" asked Pop, "how does he figure into this, other than being the cause?"

"I went to talk to him at the jail yesterday," said Max, "Higgins told me he saw an angel guarding Jim when he went in to get Mary."

"An angel?"

"Yes. An angel. He said he saw it actually bat away all the bullets."

"Wow."

"Yeah. It appears there's a lot more going on here than meets the eye."

"Daddy?"

"Yes, Mary?"

"Didn't you see the angel?"

"No, sweetie, why do you ask?"

"Because I could see him when he came in with Mister Jim. He was big and shiny, just like in my Sunday School books."

"You saw the angel?"

"Yes, daddy. That's why I was never afraid. I knew Jesus was watching over me and Mister Jim."

Max and the others just looked at each other in disbelief. They had always talked about the angels around them, but none of them had ever seen one. Sometimes it felt like it was a fable they were talking about, something for the Old Testament times but not for today. Yet they now had two different people that could testify there were indeed angels among them. That thought was still fresh in Max's mind when Dr. Bergey approached the group.

"Hello, Max, it's good to see you again. I wanted to be sure you were all here together before I said a few things. Folks, I wish I had better news, but I'm afraid we're coming close to a time when decisions must be made. Mr. Dunning's condition is gradually declining and the time is approaching when a decision must be made about removing life support and perhaps making organ donations. I know this is hard to hear and a hard decision to make. It doesn't have to be decided right now, there's time for you to all discuss it among yourselves."

Joshua had been quiet, with his back to the group, but after hearing the doctor's report, his back straightened up and he turned to face everyone.

"I've already made my decision," Joshua said, as he took the Jesus rock from his pocket and held it up for them all to see.

"Where'd that come from?" asked Brandon, "I thought it was lost forever."

"I was with Jim when he threw it away into Coal Creek. I went looking for it, and it took me a while to find it, but here it is and I'm going to put it in Jim's room so it's the first thing he sees when he wakes up."

"What is that thing?" asked Bob Korreck.

"It's a long story," answered Pop, "we'll have to fill you in on it later."

Max looked at Dr. Bergey and spoke, "I appreciate what you've done doctor, and I respect your opinion, but I think I speak for the group when I say we're going to get a second opinion and put this in the hands of the Master Physician."

Dr. Bergey smiled, "I expected this would be your response. From a professional standpoint, I can't say that I endorse it, but from a personal standpoint, I'm in your corner and I'll be praying like I'm sure you all will be doing."

"Yes we will, doctor. I wasn't sure how this morning's service was going to go, but I think the Holy Spirit has shown me the way. After we're done praying here, we're going to the church for a good, old-fashioned prayer meeting. We're going to lift up Jim's needs before the Lord and ask for Him to give us protection by the angels around us."

The next time Dr. Bergey passed by Big Jim's room everyone was already gone, but he could see the Jesus rock on the table facing Big Jim. There was something else there that made Dr. Bergey do a double-take. There, tucked under Big Jim's huge right arm, was Mary's rag doll. What the doctor's eyes couldn't see was the very large angel with his sword drawn guarding Big Jim.

Max took his place in front of the congregation, unsure of what was going to take place. Everything was quiet. He had his carefully prepared sermon notes handy, but he could feel something different was going to happen on this morning. He knew this morning belonged to the Holy Spirit and to the angels worshiping around them. He only wished there were more people there to share in it.

Things were different over at Pastor Messner's church. The people coming in were lively and chatting it up as they entered. Pastor Messner was happy as he walked up to his church, seeing so many people attending, yet he felt an emptiness inside. The Sunday attendance had nearly doubled with a lot of people starting to come over from Max's church. Pastor Messner hadn't really given that detail too much thought, but that was about to change as he approached the area where his wife, Margaret, was greeting people. What he overheard as he walked by struck a chord in his spirit.

"Yes," said Margaret, "it's wonderful that Pastor Carson got his little girl back. I know I shouldn't say it, and it's a shame he might not pull through, but that terrible man is getting what he deserves, he and that friend of his who was doing all the stealing. This will be a nice community for our families again with those evil men out of the picture."

Those words were still ringing in Pastor Messner's ears as he walked up to his pulpit. As he sat down and looked out at the congregation filtering in and nearly filling up the pews, he couldn't get it out of his head. Evil men. One of those evil men took a bullet just to save his life. That same evil man was probably going to lose his life because he drug himself out of a hospital bed to save a little girl. An evil man that said he was a follower of Jesus. Because that young man had been portrayed as an evil man by his wife Margaret, this very congregation was much larger. All for a lie. Margaret Messner had made her way to the front of the church and had taken her traditional seat at the piano, ready for the service to begin. Pastor Messner looked at the smug smile on his wife's face and immediately felt contempt for it. He could not deny the knots that were forming in his stomach and spirit as he started the service.

"Folks let's start by reading...." Pastor Messner's voice was shaking as it trailed off. Members of the congregation started to look at one another and whisper back and forth wondering what was happening. Pastor Messner put his notes aside and started again.

"Ladies and gentlemen, I apologize if you came here expecting the usual sermon. I cannot lie to you, I came here expecting to deliver the usual Sunday morning service. I don't talk much about God's Holy Spirit here, but this morning it is coming down on me so hard I can't deny it. The intentional evil that so many people practice against one another for the sole purpose of causing pain is a sure sign that the devil is real and active in our world today. On the other side of town, there's a young man fighting for his life in the hospital. Some of you know him. Word has been going around that he's a bad man who we shouldn't be around and who shouldn't be around us. Recently, that bad man not only saved the life of a little girl, but he also saved my life. Jesus gave His life for us in much the same way. That young man is not Jesus, but I now believe that Jesus is living inside him and is the reason he was willing to risk his life for others. Those of you that started to come to this church to get away from this man should prayerfully consider your decision. You're welcome to keep attending here, but search your hearts and spirits to see what church you really belong in. Jesus accepted people as they are and we should accept that young man as our Christian brother if he makes it out of that hospital alive. It's wrong to reject him or anyone else just because they look different. If I find out that anyone here has said another bad word or gossips against that young man, they'll have to answer to me."

Pastor Messner shot an icy glance at Margaret when he said that last sentence. She met his glance with anger at first, but the anger faded as his icy glare only intensified with her defiance.

"Again, I apologize to everyone expecting the normal service. Right now, I am going to leave this pulpit and walk right over to Pastor Carson's church and ask his forgiveness for any damage the false accusations against that young man may have caused his church. I invite any of you who are able and want to, to join me. We can join together in praying for that young man along the way."

A few of the older people that weren't able to walk remained behind, but almost everyone else got up and followed Pastor Messner out the door and down the street. It was a strange spectacle, one that none of the townspeople had ever seen before. A couple people in the town even followed along to see what was going on and what all the excitement was about.

In his church, Max had just finished telling the story of Dwain Higgins and the angel. He wasn't quite sure what he was going to say next when the doors at the rear of the sanctuary opened up wide to show Pastor Messner with a crowd of people behind him.

"Please forgive me for interrupting your service, Pastor Carson," said Pastor Messner, "but I got a swift kick from the Holy Spirit and felt compelled to come over here and ask your forgiveness."

"Forgiveness for what?"

"I allowed vicious lies to be told about your friend, Mr. Dunning. Those lies not only damaged him, but it hurt others and your congregation as well. We all know that young man saved my life and risked his own again to save your daughter. That pretty well proves those accusations were not true. He is a good man and our Christian brother. If you will forgive me, my congregation and I would like to come in here and join yours to pray together for that young man's healing."

Max left his pulpit and walked down the aisle to meet Pastor Messner. No words were exchanged between the two as Max looked him in the eye and then gave him a big hug.

"I forgive you, my brother. Let's put it all behind us and pray for some major healing to take place. Not just for Jim, but for our churches and community as well."

Pastor Messner was choked up with emotion and could only nod in agreement as the tears began to flow. Everyone that had come with Pastor Messner crowded into the church and began praying with those that were already there. Some people were praying individually and others were in small groups, but everyone was praying. Everyone was so wrapped up in their prayers that nobody noticed Joshua walking over to Max and whispering in his ear. Max nodded and went back up to the pulpit.

"Excuse me, folks, but Joshua here has felt a move of the Spirit. His biblical namesake took the city of Jericho by marching around it as God instructed him to. Joshua feels led to go to the hospital and march around the hospital until Jim improves. I intend on joining him and I ask that anyone else here that feels led to march with us to come along. Just like the old Bible School song, we're all in the Lord's Army and I say we fight this thing."

After a chorus of hearty "amens" everyone started heading to the hospital to march.

23
THE WALLS OF JERICHO

The hospital had never seen a mob scene like this before. Joshua had arrived first and started walking around the hospital praying for Jim. Then, one by one, carloads of people showed up and joined in the march. Bob Korreck was waiting for Max when he got there.

"I got to hand it to you Max, when you guys do something, you do it up right."

"I can't take any of the credit, Bob. Joshua was led to do this. It's amazing to see the Holy Spirit at work."

"I never heard anything about this spirit stuff when I went to church years ago. This seems so much more real than anything I've ever been around before."

"It is real, Bob. Some people say they have to see things to believe it, but usually when we're dealing with God it's the other way around, he usually shows us things after we believe."

"God really does do things in a mysterious way, eh? Anyway, Pop and I talked and he and I are going to be in Jim's room praying while all of you folks are out here marching. We figure we could do more good by praying inside."

"That's fine, Bob. That way you can come out and give us any updates too."

Pop and Bob were amazed at the group of people marching around the hospital. They guessed there were at least one hundred people marching around the hospital.

"Did you ever see anything like this Pop?"

"No, Bob, I never have. But then, I've seen lots of extraordinary things ever since Jimmy's been back in my life."

"I see the way your eyes are misting, Pop. We're not giving up Jim without a good, praying fight! Say, could I ask a favor of you?"

Pop wiped a tear from his eye. "Sure Bob, what is it?"

"Would it be okay with you if I spent a minute alone with Jim?"

"Sure Bob. Take all the time you want."

Bob stepped quietly into the room although he didn't know why. He would like nothing more to be able to wake Jim up from his coma. He cast a curious look around the room, trying to figure out what each piece of equipment was doing. Then he looked at Big Jim lying in the bed. Even unconscious he was still an imposing figure. Yet, there was a peaceful glow about him. Bob leaned closer to Big Jim to talk.

"Jim. It's Bob. I don't know if you can hear me or not, but I have to say this. I want you to know I accepted Jesus because of you. I'm all in. You made Jesus real for me and now I'm seeing Him work through His people here and now. Joshua is outside right now marching around this place and praying with a whole bunch of people. He's fighting for your healing and so am I. Thank you for leading me to salvation, Jim. Now if you don't mind, I'm going to let your old man in here and the two of us are going to war praying for you."

Bob went to the door and motioned for Pop to come into the room. They each pulled over a chair close to Big Jim so they could lay their hands on him as they prayed. The people outside prayed their hearts out too. And nothing happened. Three weeks later, Bob and Pop were still there at Big Jim's side. Joshua was still making a daily march around the hospital, but there were fewer people with him. There were usually different people every day to join him, a few even coming from other towns after they heard about the prayer march. Some of the original marchers had given up completely, thinking God's answer to their prayers was to take Big Jim home. Joshua was not about to give up and neither was Pop or Bob. Even when Dr. Bergey came in to give them the bad news.

"Hello Pop. Hello Bob."

"Hi doc, what's up?"

"This is just about the hardest thing I've ever had to do. We can't prolong this any longer. The machines are all that's keeping Jim alive."

Pop dropped his head and spoke softly. "Get Brandon, Joshua, and Max. They'd want to be here."

The mood was somber inside the room as they all gathered. This was something none of them had been expecting and it was hard.

"I'll wait for each of you to say your final good-byes before I power down the equipment," said Dr. Bergey quietly.

They looked silently at each other, none of them wanting to be first to say good-bye to Big Jim. It was then that Joshua spoke up.

"I'm not giving up. There will never be any miracles if we don't expect them. You guys can say good-bye if you want, but I'll be here praying for healing through this."

"I'm with you Joshua," said Max.

"We all are," said Brandon.

Each one of them placed their hands on Big Jim and prayed as Dr. Bergey powered down all the life-support equipment. They were still praying as they heard Dr. Bergey start moving around quickly through the room like something was happening.

"Is something wrong doc?" asked Max.

"I've powered everything down. But Mr. Dunning is still going. He's breathing on his own. His heart rate has picked up. Blood Pressure's good."

"Are you saying this is a miracle?" asked Joshua.

"I'm not saying anything, but it sure looks that way to me," said Dr. Bergey.

"Big dummy doesn't even know how to die right," chuckled Brandon through his tears.

"I don't know about that, Brandon, but it does appear that somewhere in there, he hasn't forgotten how to live," said Dr. Bergey. "This changes everything. I'll have to ask you folks to leave the room while I check things out. We'll have to keep a real close eye on Jim right now."

"I need to get back outside and tell my marchers the good news," said Joshua. "We'll have to keep marching till Jim wakes up."

"That sounds like a good idea," said Max, "let them know they're all a part of this victory."

"Why?" Everyone suddenly stopped what they were doing to listen and see if what they heard was real or they imagined it. The ragged-sounding voice had come from the bed. They were almost afraid to look, but when they did look, there was Big Jim looking back at them.

"Jim!" they all exclaimed at once. Tears of joy were flowing freely from everyone, even Dr. Bergey.

"Why?" said Big Jim again.

"What is it Jim?" asked Max, "what are you asking?"

"Why am I holding this doll?" he said as he picked up the rag doll Mary had left with him. That made everyone laugh.

"Big ugly's back for sure!" exclaimed Brandon.

Two weeks later, Big Jim had gotten strong enough to be released from the hospital. He was still not strong enough to walk out under his own power, but he was more than happy enough for someone to wheel him out in a wheelchair just to get out. He was excited that his first outing was going to be the Sunday morning church service. Max and Joshua were on their way over to pick him up and he could hardly wait. Max had told him all about Dwain's story about the angel and how Joshua led a group of people in a march around the hospital. He was so proud of Joshua's faith, so happy that this incident had led Dwain to salvation. He couldn't wait to praise God for everything that had taken place and testify publicly about everything God's grace had done for him. He was all dressed and ready to go when Max and Joshua showed up.

"I see you're ready and waiting for us Jim," said Max.

"I'm ready to get out of this place and hopefully never come back unless it's to visit someone else."

"No doubt. We'll let Joshua wheel you out of here. I'd probably end up wrecking you and you'd get hurt and have to stay."

"Don't need that happening. I thoroughly trust the driving ability of the guy who brought down the walls of Jericho."

"I didn't do anything special Jim," said Joshua, "it was all God."

"All God working through you, Joshua. It would have been a different story if you hadn't submitted yourself to serve God and lead the march around the building," said Jim.

"I didn't do anything you wouldn't have done."

"Maybe. But I wasn't there to do anything and you stepped up. I can't thank you enough."

"Yes you can, and you already have thanked me enough so it's time to move on to something else."

"Whatever you say, buddy. Let's get out of here."

It seemed like they were at the church in no time. Jim was savoring each sight and sound of the trip as if he had never experienced any of it before. All the colors seemed to be more intense than they ever had before. He could smell the flowers along the sidewalk as Joshua pushed him inside. This was almost like being born again. Jim wasn't prepared for what he saw next. As Joshua pushed the wheelchair through the doors into the sanctuary, Big Jim saw the seats were not only full, but everyone started to stand up and clap. He felt more than a little uncomfortable with that, but there wasn't any way he could run away. As they got closer to the front, he saw some of the kids that had showed up for the youth meeting he helped Max with. Each one of them was holding a small sign that said "WIN FREE SEX" and smiling. When he got closer, he could see the signs were modified from his original sign to read, "We WIN, Our salvation is FREE, but paid for by Christ, SEX is God's gift for marriage." The kids had learned what he wanted them to, and that made him proud of them.

"What do you think of all this, Jim? Pretty crazy, huh?" asked Joshua.

"Wheel me up to the front by Max, would you? I think I'm supposed to say something."

Joshua wheeled Big Jim up the side ramp to the pulpit and left him there beside Max.

"Max, I think I'm supposed to say something, do you mind?"

"You go right ahead, Jim. If you're being led by the spirit, there's no way I'm going to stop you."

Big Jim slowly got up from his wheelchair and used the pulpit to hold his weight. He felt a little nervous as he looked out over everyone, but it was something he knew he had to do. He cleared his throat and began to speak. "Hey, everybody. In case someone out there doesn't know, my name is Jim Dunning. I've been through some tough times lately that put me out of commission for a while and took me away from here. I learned something from all of this though, and I need to share it with you. I had started to think that God wasn't with me because the more I looked around the more and more I saw evil growing everywhere and I was getting discouraged. It's not that there's more evil in the world today. It's just that we're allowing less God in the world. We have to invite him into our lives to be a part of it. People out there aren't inviting him in and they don't fear the judgment, either. They're just doing whatever they want. If we don't have God in our lives, we're left on our own to fight the evil within us with our own conscience, and we'll never be strong enough to fight it off on our own. Not without God's help. He was always there with me the whole time through all my trials, I just couldn't see it. I wasn't feeling it. Apostle Paul said faith, hope, and love abides with us and the greatest is love. Well, I got to experience the love God has for us. I have it on good authority that God sent an angel to watch over me. That's just a sign of the love God has for all of us. It's our duty to take that love and the message of His grace out into the world. It will be tough, and you'll face trials, but remember, God will always be there with you. In Second Corinthians Chapter One, Paul also talked about trials he faced, about having hardship, being under great pressure, and despairing of life. I know what I went through was nothing like what Paul was facing, but it gave me an idea of how he felt. He also goes on to tell us why we have these trials when he says 'But this happened that we might not rely on ourselves but on God.' That's what it's all about. We need to rely on God in good times and bad. He's always there for us through everything."

Max got up and helped Jim back into his wheelchair. "I couldn't have said it any better myself, Jim," said Max, "I couldn't have said it any better myself."

No one could see them, but a chorus of angels that was surrounding the congregation raised their swords in a salute.

ABOUT THE AUTHOR

The author lives in southern Pennsylvania with his family and an assortment of animals. Included with the menagerie are four children who are in various stages of living their lives.

If you liked this book, please read
"The Jesus Rock"
also by D.L. Ford
and see how this story started!

31433847R00111

Made in the USA
Charleston, SC
16 July 2014